Deadly Force

He heard the crackling of the shot before he felt it tear through his back and explode out his chest. The force of the impact sent him flying forward. He tried to put his hands out to block his fall, but his arms didn't work anymore.

And in the seconds before his head smashed into the desert rock, he realized that he and Ryan were part of a hunt, but not the kind of hunt they had planned for their leave.

Clowes had never been prey before.

And he finally, in the last moment of his life, understood why prey usually lost.

Don't miss any of these exciting *Aliens, Predator,* and *Aliens vs. Predator* adventures from Bantam Books!

Aliens #1: Earth Hive by Steve Perry
Aliens #2: Nightmare Asylum by Steve Perry
Aliens #3: The Female War by Steve Perry and Stephani Perry

Aliens: Genocide by David Bischoff
Aliens: Alien Harvest by Robert Sheckley
Aliens: Rogue by Sandy Schofield
Aliens: Labyrinth by S. D. Perry
Aliens: Music of the Spears by Yvonne Navarro

Aliens vs. Predator: Prey by Steve Perry and Stephani Perry
Aliens vs. Predator: Hunter's Planet by David Bischoff

Predator: Concrete Jungle by Nathan Archer
Predator: Cold War by Nathan Archer
Predator: Big Game by Sandy Schofield

PREDATOR™

BIG GAME

BY
Sandy Schofield

Based on the Dark Horse graphic novel of the same name.

SCRIPT BY
John Arcudi

BANTAM BOOKS
New York Toronto London Sydney Auckland

PREDATOR: BIG GAME
A Bantam Spectra Book / February 1999

SPECTRA and the portrayal of a boxed "s" are trademarks
of Bantam Books, a division of Random House, Inc.

ISBN 0-553-57733-6

Published simultaneously in the United States and Canada

Bantam Books are published by Bantam Books, a division of
Random House, Inc. Its trademark, consisting of the words
"Bantam Books" and the portrayal of a rooster, is Registered
in U.S. Patent and Trademark Office and in other countries.
Marca Registrada. Bantam Books, 1540 Broadway, New York,
New York 10036.

PRINTED IN THE UNITED STATES OF AMERICA

OPM   10 9 8 7 6 5 4 3 2 1

For Bill Trojan

PREDATOR™

BIG GAME

1

f asked, Enoch Nakai would say he has no brother. And he would be telling the truth. Yet I am his brother. I am Navajo, just as he is. I died in childbirth, a twin that was seldom talked about. Since that day I have remained in the world of my ancestors, watching over my brother, as I would have done if I had lived. I am Tobadjishchini, *the one who distracts the monster while my brother kills it.*

Enoch Nakai, my brother, is the Nayenezgani, *the monster slayer.* The Navajo sing songs of our deeds. They have for centuries. They sang of future events and did not know it. Often, for my people, the difference between past, present, and future is not important.

But now is the future. It has arrived with one twin alive and the other only a spirit. I stand ready, even though my brother does not yet know of his place or his duty.

This is the story of how the monster is fought. This is how it starts.

. . .

The scattered mesas had lonely duty over the dark New Mexico night. The slight gold in the western sky was a faint reminder of the long, hot day; the silver in the eastern sky the promise of a cold night, soon to be guarded by a full moon. But for now the rocks, the red sand, the brush stood mute as the blackness crept in over the high desert and arroyos that twisted between the scattered rock mesas. Above it all the sky was peppered with thousands of stars, casting very little light on the animals and insects that hunted in the magic time between day and night.

Near the base of one small mesa, a puma crouched on the warmth of a flat rock, its huge golden eyes watching a small group of wild boar feed among the scrub. The cat's fur was the dusty color of the red-and-gold desert dirt, brush, and sand. When not moving, the cat was almost invisible.

Not a muscle twitched as it waited. It was a patient hunter. It wouldn't attack the entire group. Even with its speed, strength, and razor-sharp claws, it wouldn't stand a chance against the pointed tusks of five boar. Boar were nasty creatures, often not worth the effort it took to kill one. The cat had been injured once, a long time ago, by a wild boar. It had never forgotten the pain. Since then, it had killed dozens of boar, but always cautiously, carefully, never making the same mistake twice.

As it had done many nights before, the big cat watched for the chance that one of the boar might stray just a little too far from the rest. Then the cat would take its prize.

Until that moment came, the cat would wait.

It didn't have to wait long.

A very faint breeze, still warm from the day's sun, brought the odor of boar downwind. A boar was close. It was snuffling, searching for something that smelled good in the dirt. The cat watched.

Behind the cat, the first sliver of the full moon broke above a nearby mesa, casting faint silver shadows among the scrub and rock. The cat didn't move as the boar rooted, making enough noise to attract a dozen other hunters. But in this instance, only the big cat waited.

Suddenly the stars above the desert were shoved into the background by a bright light. Then the quiet of the night was overpowered by a thunderous roar.

Not more than a few hundred feet over the boar pack, a black shape flashed past, rustling the brush and swirling up small clouds of red sand and dust. In its wake, it left a wind that smelled of metal and the tang of fuel.

The cat remained deathly still, its eyes only slits.

All of the boar squealed in fright and broke into the brush, scattering as if the shape in the sky had landed in their midst instead of just passing over. The big cat, ignoring what had happened among the stars, moved, placing itself between the stray boar and the rest of the pack, cutting off any retreat. The boar, already panicked from the light and noise, now smelled the cat. The beast ran, squealing and snorting, moving farther away from the others and the safety of numbers. If it were cornered, it would turn and fight. It would kill if it had to.

The sky above had returned to normal, and after what seemed only a moment the desert seemed to forget that anything had interrupted the normal course of the night.

But events had changed. Soon the cat would feed. The cat ran after the single boar, steadily, silently, making no mistake, remaining hidden, even as it gave chase.

On a slight ridgeline just above the big cat another figure stepped up, surveying the surrounding desert as if it owned it. This figure did not belong in the high desert. Its massive, humanlike shape was alien to everything around it. But like the cat, it too was a hunter. And now it stood silently, watching the cat follow the boar through the rocks and brush.

The moon had risen higher, gloriously full. If the cat had looked up from the desert floor, it would have seen the figure outlined against that bright circle. The moon illuminated the intruder's shape and reflected off the armor on the knees, thighs, arms, shoulders, and head. Thick claws extended from its fingers and toes, and thick snakelike strands of hair hung from under its almost flat-topped helmet. A necklace of bones hung around its neck, draping over its chest.

But because it was downwind, the big cat missed the creature looming above it. Instead, the cat's attention was focused completely on the boar. The boar had settled down slightly, thinking it had lost its pursuer. The boar still smelled of fear, but the scent was receding. The cat crouched, motionless. The boar was about to make its first and final mistake.

The boar glanced over its shoulder, saw and smelled no predator, and then rooted in the dirt. The cat's muscles tensed. It was about to spring, to tear out the boar's throat in one massive bite, when suddenly a blue bolt hissed through the air like a snake striking.

The big cat froze as the snaking energy struck the boar just under the head and exploded, killing the prey instantly.

The cat had seen animals die like that only once, when humans were present. And the cat knew that if the human saw it, the cat would die too. So the big cat turned and vanished silently into the brush and rock.

But the cat was wrong. There were no humans. The only two-legged being was the alien above, the alien watching the cat as it went, nearly invisible against the darkened landscape. The alien nodded with approval. One hunter always appreciates the skills of another. Then the alien moved down to the body of the boar and, with a quick slice of a hidden blade, cut its neck. It held the bloody head up in the air, as if offering the prize to some unseen god among the stars.

Then, hooking the boar's head onto its belt, the alien started off through the rocks and desert brush, moving silently through the darkness.

The big cat also moved on, searching for new prey.

The smell of the boar's fresh blood would bring out the desert scavengers to clean up the remains of the kill. Within three days there would be nothing remaining but scattered white bones, bleaching in the heat of the day. Thus was the way of the high desert.

The alien glanced in the cat's direction, tempted

by hunting such an experienced hunter. But in the end, the alien decided to move toward its primary target. There was an enclave of humans not far from here. They, the alien knew, were worthy prey.

They would give him a challenging hunt.

2

I, Enoch's silent brother, watched the arrival of the monster, standing on a low mesa. As a spirit I could not feel the warm breeze, or smell the blood from the boar, yet I could imagine such sensations as I watched. Just as the boar was not aware of the cat, and the cat was not aware of the monster, the monster was not aware I watched. I am no threat to the monster. Only my brother can face him, as our ancestors have decided. The stories were all true, even though they were of the future.

Like the big cat, at the time of the monster's arrival, my brother was also unaware of many things, including his destiny. But soon he would be forced to face his true nature.

Due east, two miles from where the cat had hunted, Cole Army Base filled a round valley, tucked under surrounding mesas and low rolling hills. The lights of the base pushed back the night, covering the nearby desert with a faint orange-and-white glow.

Corporal Enoch Nakai stood at ease in front of Sergeant Coates's desk, listening, as the sergeant mumbled something about a duty roster and shuffled through a pile of papers on the corner of the old wooden desk. Nakai had never been in the sergeant's office that late at night, and the room seemed even smaller than normal. The place was always about five degrees too hot, and tonight was no exception. The walls had a dingy yellow tint, and everything reeked of cigar smoke. A picture of the president hung crookedly on one wall, revealing a clean patch behind the frame, making the room's filth even more apparent.

Nakai liked the open air and cool winds of the desert. He couldn't imagine why any man would keep himself cooped up in such a room.

"Ah, here it is," the sergeant said, yanking a paper out of the pile.

Nakai knew, without a doubt, what the sergeant was going to say: Nakai's three-day leave had been canceled. Again. There was no other reason the sergeant would have called him in this close to lights out.

"I'm afraid I've got to cancel your leave, Corporal," the sergeant said, right on cue. "I need you on tank duty tomorrow morning sharp."

Nakai remained at ease, although he could feel his muscles tense. This leave was important to him. He had made promises, promises he thought he could deliver on. He had figured that the sarge could pick on him only for so long.

Apparently, he was wrong.

"Sir," Nakai said. "I put in for that leave three weeks ago."

The sergeant shrugged and tossed the paper back on top of the pile. "No one ever said the army was going to be perfect, did they, Corporal?"

There was no hope, Nakai knew, of changing the sergeant's mind. The man had no intention of letting him go.

"No, sir," Nakai said, keeping his face calm and without a sign of emotion. He had practiced such an expression hundreds of times in front of mirrors, and he knew exactly what it looked like. He wouldn't give the sergeant even a hint of emotion to fuel his petty game. "Permission to be excused, sir?"

The sergeant hesitated for just a moment, then nodded. "Granted."

Nakai spun and left, moving quickly out of the command barracks. He felt as if he would suffocate in there. That tiny office stank like the sarge. Nakai inhaled a lungful of fresh desert air, just laced with the night's chill, and then blew out the foul stench of the sarge's office. The small ritual, usually effective, didn't help, and Nakai knew why.

He was nervous. Alda was going to be really mad at him, even though this wasn't his fault. She had been planning for this leave for weeks and she didn't take a change in plans well at all. She never had. And he had made this one worse by promising. When would he learn?

Alda worked as a waitress at Ben's Saloon in the small town of Agate, New Mexico, about forty minutes from the base. Like Nakai, she was Native, with long black hair and dark eyes that seemed to look right through a person. At best she stood no more than five feet tall and didn't weigh more than a wet horse blanket, yet she was the strongest and most powerful woman he had ever met. No one at Ben's messed with her.

For some reason that Nakai couldn't fathom, she loved him, and had stuck with him through the worst of his drinking, and his first year in the service. And every time he got really down, or started dwelling on the dark memories of his early days as an orphan, she would find a way to bring him back to the present. She was the best thing that had ever happened to him, and he knew it.

He did his best not to screw things up, and somehow that wasn't enough. He was going to have to cancel out on yet another leave. She wasn't going to understand.

His stomach twisted and he felt a familiar thirst. Instead, he clenched his fist, and rehearsed what he would say. He closed his eyes for a brief moment.

It would sound like he was making excuses. She hadn't believed him the last time. She had exacted the promise then. And like an idiot, he had made it.

I won't plan anything with you if it's not for sure, Alda. I promise that my next leave will happen. We'll do anything you want.

Yeah. Anything. Except be together.

He cursed the sergeant silently. Army life could be so good under the right commander. Nakai had seen it. He had seen how a well-run unit behaved.

But the sarge was not the right leader for him. The man delighted in making Nakai miserable. And even when Nakai didn't show his misery, the sarge somehow knew.

Nakai glanced at his watch. He had fifteen minutes until lights-out, time for one quick call.

The evening air swirled around him as he cut across the open ground in the center of the camp and into the mess. Inside, the heat of the day lingered, and the place actually felt humid. It smelled of grease and onions, with a faint stench of the abomination that the base called tacos. The tables were clean, but no one had washed the floor yet. Bits of meat and lettuce mixed with the dirt from unpolished boots.

Only two other soldiers were at the bank of phones along the mess wall. Nakai headed for the phone farthest on the left and dialed the saloon.

Ben answered. Nakai greeted him, and Ben didn't respond. Instead, he banged the receiver on a nearby surface and shouted over the muttered bar sounds, "It's your soldier boy."

Nakai leaned against the pay phone's sturdy metal frame. He heard faint laughter through the phone line, then the blare of an old Elvis tune from the jukebox. The receiver clattered.

"Enoch?" Alda said, worry in her voice. "Is everything all right?"

"No," Nakai said, the anger coming out a little more and a little louder than he would have liked. "My leave is canceled."

There was a moment of silence. He braced himself.

"Oh, no," Alda said faintly. "Not again."

"Again," Nakai said.

"It's been almost two months," Alda said. "I was really looking forward to seeing you."

"Look," Nakai said, forcing himself to take a deep breath. "Don't be mad. There was—"

"I'm not mad," Alda said. "Just disappointed."

Her response surprised him. She usually didn't react to change so well. But she had known of his struggles here, and she had been supporting him in all he did.

His anger at the sarge grew. It wasn't fair. He could almost hear the sarge's voice in his head: *Whoever said army life would be fair?*

No one. But a man deserved leave every once in a while.

"I'm disappointed too," Nakai said through clenched teeth. "And I'm angry."

"Don't be," Alda said. "We'll be together our entire lives. We can get through this."

Nakai didn't know what to say to that. He closed his eyes and leaned his forehead against the pay phone's cool metal. He had braced himself for the worst, and it hadn't happened. He had to stop misjudging Alda. She was the most amazing woman in the world, and he had to be the luckiest guy in the world to have her.

"Enoch?" she asked. "Are you all right?"

He opened his eyes and stood up. "I'm better now."

"Good."

He glanced at his watch. There was still a little time before he had to get back to the barracks. If he concentrated, he could pretend he was talking to Alda in person, instead of on the phone.

He asked her how her day had gone, and as she told him, he listened to the warmth in her voice, the warmth she always had when she spoke to him, the warmth he never wanted to lose.

They talked as long as they could. Nakai timed the conversation to the second to get the most out of it. Then, at a quick run, he made it back to his barracks with a full minute before lights-out.

3

It has started. The monster has come. My brother will face him today for the first time, just after sunrise, as the legends say. But today I can do nothing to help him. My time is not yet. I must wait, and watch. My brother must fight the monster alone. It is the way it was foretold by our ancestors.

The sun was just shoving the last of the night back into the cracks in the red rocks. A faint chill covered everything, and thin layers of moisture glistened on the nearby yucca bushes. Within an hour the sun would bake the moisture from the air and the wind would pick up, cutting at everything with fine dust and sand. But for the moment, as the sun cleared the distant mountains, the night hunters were gone, the air was still cool and clear, and the desert felt almost comfortable.

At least, Nakai thought it comfortable. He loved

the desert at sunrise. Every smell, every sensation seemed to be intensified by the simple clarity of the air. He had lost his three-day pass, but at least he got morning tank duty. Sitting out here at this time of the morning almost made up for the loss of leave. Almost.

He leaned back against the turret of the camouflaged tank, letting the faint sun warm his face. The tank's metal was cool; in a few hours it would be too hot to touch. Nakai liked that too. He liked the predictability of the desert's weather, and its extremes. He felt as if he had been born to be in this place, at this time. He felt that way every time he had morning tank duty. Somehow, the desert called to him, reached him, was part of his soul.

Private Dietl moaned beside him. Dietl was a short, scrappy man whose crew cut made his blond hair look white. Usually the hair stood out in sharp contrast to his dark tan, but this morning Dietl's skin was paler than his hair. His eyes were red-rimmed and he shaded them as if the morning light were too much for him.

From the story Nakai had managed to get on the hike out from the base, the private had spent most of the night drinking. Where he had gotten the liquor on the base was anyone's guess, but the kid from California had a way of finding things. Last night he must have had enough booze to get himself and the others in his barracks fairly drunk. Nakai hadn't seen Dietl this hungover in the six months he had known him.

Dietl moaned again.

"Don't worry," Nakai said dryly. "It'll pass."

"I might be dead by then." Dietl leaned back

and struck his head against the turret. The dull clang echoed across the desert. Dietl raised a hand to his head. "I mean, I *will* be dead by then."

Nakai grinned and leaned back, carefully so that he wouldn't hit his own head. He liked Dietl. For some reason, the two of them had hit it off right from the start, even though they came from very different backgrounds. Nakai had been raised on the reservation by his grandfather after his mother had died in childbirth and his father drank himself to death. Dietl had been raised in a large home on a country club in Southern California. He had never worried about money or food, but had simply had everything handed to him. Yet somehow Dietl had become a fairly solid kid, reliable and respectable, without an ounce of prejudice in his body.

Dietl moaned again and Nakai's smile grew. Many mornings in the past he had felt exactly the same, too hungover even to care if the world ended. It had been nine months since he had taken a drink, thanks to Alda. And for some reason that made him feel smug, especially the more Dietl moaned.

"Oh," Dietl said, rubbing his head with both hands slowly, as if stroking an overripe tomato, "why won't this headache go away?"

"Maybe because you hit your head on the tank?"

Dietl glared at him. Just looking at Dietl's blood-shot eyes was painful. Nakai remembered exactly how it felt to be that hung over. Exactly. And he didn't ever want to feel it again.

Dietl ran his fingers through his short-cropped hair, apparently searching for the bump. "This must be why they don't want us grunts to have alcohol on the base."

"More than likely," Nakai said. "That, and loaded guns." He handed Dietl a canteen. "Drink. A lot of water helps."

Dietl groaned, but took the offered canteen and managed to get a fairly large swallow down before he choked. Then he stretched out on the top of the tank, his feet draping down over the front edge, his pack under his head as a pillow.

Nakai took the canteen back, and hung it on his belt.

"Mind if I nap?" Dietl asked. "I don't think Mama Dietl's boy is going to be any use to anyone at the moment. Wake me if the Russians attack."

Nakai only laughed as Dietl leaned his head against the pack and moaned again.

A slight breeze swirled around the tank, bringing the fresh smells of the morning desert. The heat had an odor, a dry warm odor, and so did the dirt. Slight, spicy, and very faint. And very familiar. They were all familiar smells to Nakai, smells he had loved since his childhood.

Then the wind shifted, just a little, and Nakai caught a whiff of something new. It smelled rank, like something had died out in the desert and was rotting near them.

But not really.

Nakai knew what death smelled like. He knew every odor. His grandfather had taught him how to tell, just from something's smell, how long it had been roasting in the hot desert sun.

This rank smell was familiar enough; it was wild boar, not very long dead. But beneath the odor was another one, very faint, and unfamiliar. It smelled like petroleum, old shoes, and the perfume his third cousin used to wear. It smelled like musty blankets and cinnamon. It smelled like all of that, and none of it all at the same time.

Nakai rose so that he could catch the scent better. He moved to the front of the tank, the rifle in his hands at ready, as he tried to take in every odor, every whiff of the strangeness in the air.

"Private," Nakai said, his voice low and firm. "Get up."

Dietl moaned and sat up. "What?"

"Do you smell anything?"

Dietl put a hand behind himself as a brace. "Smell something? Are you kidding? My head is so full of cotton, I couldn't smell a dead fish slapped over my nose."

"I'm telling you," Nakai said, "I smell a weird odor and it's coming from over there." He pointed to a small group of alligator juniper trees. The trees were small, almost stunted, with scaly deep brown bark.

Dietl slowly stood and moved over beside Nakai. "What's it smell like?"

Nakai let the morning air in fully, sorting the familiar from the strange odor. And the more he breathed, the more his hand tightened on the rifle.

"I can't say, exactly," Nakai said. "And that's what worries me. It's sort of like a rotting sweat, but sweeter."

"Well, it's certainly hot enough for that already," Dietl said. "And it's not even seven in the morning."

"Shhh," Nakai said, holding up his hand. "Listen."

A faint sound had come from those stunted, twisted trees. A rustle, combined with a clicking, like beads striking one another.

Nakai squinted. There was no place to hide in those branches. No real foliage to cover a person, yet he could swear that the sound he heard came from those trees. Not from beside them, but from *up in* them. And the more he focused, the more the normal sounds of the desert disappeared, leaving only the sound from the trees.

Breathing sounds.

Faint. Heavy.

The slight crack of a brittle branch.

More breathing.

Something very large was in those trees, yet Nakai's eyes told him nothing was there. The words of his grandfather came back strong.

Boy, never trust just one sense. Use them all. You will need them all.

Right now Nakai's nose and his ears said something was there, in the tree, watching them. Possibly waiting to attack.

"Someone's in those trees," Nakai whispered. "I can hear him."

Dietl scrambled to his feet, the scraping of his boots on the metal tank extraordinarily loud in the morning air. He came up beside Nakai and grinned.

"Let's see if we can send a scare into whatever's up there."

Dietl brought up his rifle and swung it in the direction of the trees, aiming as he did so.

"No!" Nakai shouted, but he was too late.

As Dietl brought up his rifle, a thin beam of flickering red light lanced from the tree and found Dietl, three bright red dots crawling over his torso. In the tree, about halfway up, the air shimmered and turned a faint blue.

"Get down!" Nakai shouted as he dove off the side of the tank.

His warning came too late.

A bolt of blue energy shot from the air in the tree, slicing Dietl directly though the chest before he even had a chance to pull the trigger. The private was dead before he hit the top of the tank.

Nakai rolled against the tread of the tank as more bolts of blue energy cut the ground near him. With each blast the air crackled and sparked, and the red dirt was burned black. A dry electric smell, like lightning in a powerful storm, seared the air.

Whatever was in that tree was invisible and firing a weapon like nothing Nakai had ever heard or seen.

Nakai rolled to the far side of the tank, then opened up on the area in the center of the tree where the shots had come from. His own rifle jerked in his hands as he fired. He steadied it, and shot again. The blue bolts kept zinging the air. He crouched, still firing, and ran low to the ground. He no longer aimed. He just shot randomly, hoping that he would hit whatever was firing at him.

His feet sank in the soft dirt, and yet he was running faster than he ever had in his life, faster than he had run when he was a teenage track star years before.

Another blast of energy cut the ground under

his feet and he stumbled, diving over a rock ledge as more bolts cut the air where he had been.

The guy in the tree was a good shot, but not perfect. Nakai was lucky.

He rolled through some scrub and rose in one quick motion, never stopping. No more surges of blue energy exploded around him as he sped off downhill, twisting and leaping, never slowing.

And as he ran, more of his grandfather's words came back to him, as clear as if the old man were speaking them now.

The monster will arrive firing death from no more than a shimmer in the air.

Nakai just wished he knew what the hell his grandfather had meant.

4

My brother is a brave man. But even the brave must know when to run away from danger. My brother is also smart. So the first time he fought the monster, he ran. It was the right thing to do. He is not stupid. Stupid men are not brave, they are simply dead.

Corporal David Winford bounced the army humvee through a shallow wash and up a rock slope, spinning the wheels in the dirt and sand. He was following what would laughingly be called a road, but in New Mexico anything less than four-wheel drive wouldn't have made it the first half mile.

The sun beat down on his freckled skin. He had forgotten his hat back at the base, possibly a serious mistake. He was a redhead, with a redhead's fair coloring, and just this brief exposure to the sun would turn him into a lobster. It had happened before.

The back of the humvee spun sideways before

the tires dug down to rock and lurched him forward. He gunned the engine just a little, giving the machine enough power to top a slight ridge. David was sweating as much from fighting the humvee over the road as he was from the early-morning sun. Even the wind rushing through his short hair didn't help cool him. And worst of all, he knew it was all going to be for nothing. The colonel and the sarge were investigating a supposed bogey landing. They had taken a half-dozen trucks and humvees this morning when they left. They certainly didn't need another. It was just another stupid make-work job. And he hated it. And he hated the army.

He spun the humvee through another wash and had just started up the other side of the ravine when a figure burst over the top of the ridge, running at full speed.

"Now what the hell?" Winford said. He slammed on the brake and watched the guy barrel down the slope, leaping over rocks and brush like a hunted deer. The guy was wearing fatigues, and looked familiar.

The guy glanced over his shoulder once before skidding to a stop beside the vehicle.

"Nakai?" Winford said, startled at the look on the man's sweat-covered face. "Aren't you supposed to be on tank duty today?"

The question came out of surprise as much as anything else. No one ran away from his post, especially not Nakai. Nakai was always being hounded by the sarge, and made up for it by following the rules to the letter. Winford respected Nakai for that; most men would have given up entirely—including Winford. After all, if he were going to be yelled at for performing his job, he might as well be a screw-off, right? At least, that's how the others would have thought. Nakai was another matter.

Nakai took a deep shuddering breath—Winford had never heard anyone's breathing sound so ragged before—and then managed to speak. "I am on duty. But I won't go back up there."

Winford's shoulders stiffened. Something was very wrong. "Why not, Corporal?"

"You don't know what I saw." Nakai never really looked at Winford, but instead kept scanning the hillside above them, watching for something he obviously thought might be chasing him.

Winford had seen that haunted look on green boys in boot camp when they realized they were in the service for the duration, but he had never seen it on a man who'd been in the army as long as Nakai. Winford had seen a pale version of that look on the faces of some of the COs, though, when they were reminiscing about Desert Storm.

Winford unlatched the safety strap on his pistol, and scanned the hillside where Nakai was staring. Nakai was making him nervous. There was nothing moving up there at all. Just sand and scrub and rock. Just exactly the same as everywhere else around the base.

"So what *did* you see?" Winford asked.

Nakai stared into Winford's eyes for a moment, then looked back up the hill. "It's something I should report directly to the sarge, or the colonel."

Something serious then. Winford inclined his head toward the empty seat beside him. "Well, then, hop aboard. I'm heading out to see 'em now."

Nakai nodded and slowly climbed into the

humvee all the time staying alert and focused on the hill he had come down. Winford looked again. He couldn't see anything.

"Seems like you lost whatever it was."

Nakai shook his head once, almost in dismissal. "It's not as simple as that."

"Seems straightforward to me," Winford said.

"Just drive," Nakai snapped.

Winford glanced at him. Nakai's reaction had nothing to do with army protocol or the chain of command. It was cold and harsh, and beneath it, Winford thought he could hear a faint tone of fear.

He ground the vehicle into motion, lurching up along the dirt road. Over the noise of the engine he said, "I'm sure the sarge is going to want to know why you're not at your post."

Corporal Nakai just stared out at the desert, looking for his unseen pursuer, not saying a word. If Nakai didn't care about the sarge's reaction, then things had to be very bad.

For the next few minutes they bounced down through an arroyo, then up the side, over more rock and dirt. Winford fought the humvee forward over the rough ground, using the directions he'd been given at the base. Nakai sat quietly, holding on through the bumps, not even seeming to notice the roughness of the ride. Instead his gaze darted from one rock to the next, one bush to the next, looking for God only knew what. Winford sure didn't. And Nakai clearly wasn't saying.

Within ten minutes they cleared the top of a high ridge near the base of a large mesa. The sight of the valley below damn near made Winford stomp on the brakes.

The trucks that had left the base that morning before sunrise were in a circle surrounding something red and brown. The thing was round, and large, but not so large that it couldn't be held by chains and lowered, with a crane, onto the back of a flatbed truck. Winford couldn't tell what the thing was, but it almost matched the New Mexico desert rock.

"What the—?" Nakai said as he stood in the moving humvee and started at the sight ahead, holding on to the top of the windshield to keep from getting tossed to the sand.

At first Winford couldn't figure out what he was looking at. Then, as he stopped the humvee just above the circle of other vehicles, he understood. The red-and-brown "something" was an aircraft. A very strange-looking circular craft, not much bigger than a pickup truck. It had race-car-like fins on one side, and a cockpit area in the center. It was clearly a one-person machine, but there was no sign of the person who had flown it.

Suddenly, from out of the group standing near the craft, the sarge's voice boomed. "Corporal Nakai. Just what the hell are you doing out here?"

Beside the sarge, Colonel Athelry turned, frowning. Athelry was a slight, wiry man, with graying hair and a graying mustache. His skin was like leather, tanned by years of exposure to the elements. The thought made Winford touch his own face. It was hot. He was going to be badly burned.

As if that mattered. The world had suddenly turned weird. Thank heaven for the sarge's predictable behavior. He was glaring at Nakai as he waited for an answer.

Nakai, still standing in the humvee, forced himself to look away from the strange craft. Then he snapped to attention and saluted.

Both the sarge and colonel stepped toward the humvee.

"Well, soldier?" the colonel said, somehow almost managing not to shout. "You were asked a question."

"Sir," Corporal Nakai said. "I must speak to you about a matter of extreme urgency."

"I'll say we have a matter of extreme urgency," the sarge shouted at him as he stopped in front of the humvee.

Winford managed to keep his hands on the steering wheel and his eyes straight ahead, trying to be as invisible as he could be as the sarge yelled at Nakai over him.

The sarge didn't give Nakai any time to answer. "There's a foreign covert aircraft in our backyard and you've *abandoned your post*!"

Winford had seen the sarge angry before, but never like this.

Nakai snapped off his salute, then climbed from the humvee and stood at attention in front of the sarge and the colonel. "Begging the sergeant's pardon," he said, "but I believe I may have encountered the occupant of that aircraft, and he's no spy, sir."

"What?" the colonel said, stepping forward and into the corporal's face.

Nakai didn't even flinch. "I said, sir, that he's no spy."

Winford froze. Nakai was running scared from the person who came in that craft? Winford almost turned toward Nakai. But to do that would be to call attention to himself which, at this moment, was probably not a good thing to do.

The colonel stared at Nakai for a long minute, never moving his gaze from Nakai's face. Then the colonel glanced at the sarge and nodded.

"Winford," the sarge said, "leave the humvee here and see what you can do to help load that craft on the trucks."

Winford climbed quickly out of the vehicle.

"Yes, sir," he said, hoping he kept the disappointment out of his voice. Winford had been a small part of this drama, but no one felt he deserved to know what happened. That was one of his greatest frustrations of army life: he never got to know the full details about anything—and it seemed like this was something to know about.

Winford turned and headed down the hill. It was clear to him that the sarge and colonel had ideas as to what the pilot of this craft might be. And it sounded as if Nakai's information contradicted theirs.

A spy craft?

A space craft?

Could it be both?

Winford shivered despite the growing heat. He glanced over his shoulder. No one was watching him. He lingered, hoping to hear what was going on.

"Okay, son," the colonel said to Nakai "Tell us what you saw."

Nakai nodded once, and spoke. But Winford was too far away to hear his answer.

5

My brother tried to warn those who command him about the monster. My brother had remembered our grandfather's words. Those in charge did not believe him, did not want to listen to our grandfather's warnings. But my brother did not speak of a matter of belief. He spoke of truth. Truth may or may not be believed, but that does not alter truth. Truth is. Speakers of truth understand that. They also understand that truth always wins, but sometimes with the winning comes death.

The sun was low in the pale blue sky, just an orange ball above the western hills, but the day's heat still covered everything like a thick blanket on a warm night. Private Nathaniel Clowes held his M-16 in ready position across his chest as he crouched near the front of the tank. Sweat dripped off his forehead and he could feel it soaking his undershirt. It would be a relief when the cool of the night finally arrived.

He wiped his face with the back of his hand, his knuckles scraping against the cap he had worn backward since he got out of boot camp. It was his signature, his way of being different in this place where conformity was prized. A number of commanders had tried to get him to wear a regulation hat, but he never did. All of the commanders learned, quickly, not to make the cap an issue. It was one of the few things that Clowes felt strongly about.

Right now the cap felt like a talisman. Something was making him uneasy here, something he couldn't quite put a finger on.

Neither could his partner, Corporal Ryan. At least that was what Ryan had said as they approached the tank. But their voices had dropped to whispers, and finally they had stopped speaking altogether. Ryan was beside the tank now, holding his own M-16 muzzle upward as he inspected the scrub-covered sand and the small stand of trees. Clowes glanced at him. Ryan shrugged, meaning he had found nothing.

Yet.

Ryan was a tall, thin kid who had joined up right out of high school. He had reddish-brown hair, chopped short, and brown eyes that seemed always to have a touch of humor in them. He could pull practical jokes with the best of them. Clowes knew that all too well, since he had been the butt of a number of them.

But Ryan didn't seem to be in a joking mood now. He had his head tilted back slightly, as if he were trying to identify something by smell. If anyone could do that, Ryan could. He was from the woods of Oregon, and had been raised to hunt. Clowes had been raised in West Texas, and knew a bit about hunting himself. In fact, it was while telling hunting stories that the two men had become friends. They were planning to take their next two leaves together as part of a bet: Ryan said hunting was better in Oregon. Clowes claimed it was better in Texas. They would go to Oregon first, Texas second. And when those two leaves were over, Clowes knew he would have fifty dollars of Ryan's money. Nothing—especially not a spotted-owl-filled rain forest—beat West Texas.

The wind shifted slightly, and Clowes winced. Something smelled wrong, but he'd caught only a sense of it, not a full-fledged sniff. He held his gun tighter. He and Ryan were alone, though. Clowes had an intuition about that, and it rarely failed him.

He didn't know how he'd tell the sarge that they couldn't locate Dietl. Sarge didn't like anything untidy. Clowes was willing to give this search an extra effort just to avoid the sarge's wrath.

Not that they had finished examining the area. They hadn't even been to the other side of the tank yet.

This whole assignment had Clowes nervous. The sarge had pulled him aside—*him*, not Ryan—and warned him to take all precautions. Then the sarge had gotten just a hair too close to him, and whispered that he believed Private Dietl had been killed out here and that he wanted them to investigate. Real "hush-hush" for the moment. He didn't tell Clowes what might have killed Dietl. And when asked, the sarge had simply said, "Go look and you tell me."

Clowes had asked Ryan if the sarge had told him the same thing. Ryan merely looked at him with that cold humorless gaze that he reserved for moments when someone asked him something stupid.

"If the sarge said it was hush-hush," Ryan had said, "then it's hush-hush."

The only thing Clowes could conclude was that the sarge didn't care if they worked together. He just wanted them to find whatever they could.

Whatever that meant.

"Anything?" Clowes asked softly.

"Nothing," Ryan said.

But neither of them had moved from their positions. This tank had been manned nearly twenty-four hours a day since Clowes had been in camp. Having it now sit unmanned like this seemed almost unnatural, and unnerving.

The sun clipped the top of the nearby mesa and the evening breeze kicked harder, swirling dust and hot air. The smell that had been teasing Clowes became a full-blown odor: the stench of rot and decay that brought Sarge's warning completely to mind. The smell instantly twisted Clowes's stomach, forcing him to swallow.

"You smell that?" Ryan asked, moving slowly around in front of the tank. He still held his M-16 upright, as if he had a flag hanging off it. Clowes wished Ryan would hold the damn thing properly. Something was wrong here, and it would be better if they both were prepared.

"Yeah, I smell that." Clowes stood, but stayed in his position. "What the hell is it?"

"Blood," Ryan said, pointing the barrel of his gun at the front of the tank. "And lots of it."

Blood. Clowes felt his unease grow stronger. And that sixth sense of his was kicking up. There was something nearby. Something watching them. He glanced over his shoulder, but saw nothing except more scrub and sand.

Slowly, he walked forward, stopping beside Ryan. The stench was stronger here. It made Clowes's eyes water. He wiped them with his dirty left thumb, keeping a solid grip on his weapon with his right.

"See?" Ryan asked.

The fading sunlight bounced off the front of the tank, and Clowes had to squint in order to see. It took a moment for his eyes to adjust. Then he realized his eyes weren't the problem. What he was seeing as a shadow on the tank's front wasn't shadow at all. It was blood. Black, dried blood, covering most of the tank. Hundreds of flies were swarming in a thick puddle on the tank's top.

"Shit," Clowes whispered.

"If he bled that much," Ryan said, his voice trembling just a little, "where could he have gone?"

Clowes took a step forward. Think of it as if the blood were not human. Think of it like he would if he were hunting.

He peered at the area around the blood. A trail moved off toward the trees, a trail of spattered blood. This wasn't the trail left by something wounded running away to a place of safety. This was a trail made by something else, carrying away the wounded. Nothing could bleed like that and move on its own.

"Here." Clowes used his own gun to point at the trail.

Ryan stepped beside him, his voice naturally low. "You think maybe Nakai killed him?"

Clowes looked at his partner. Ryan's brown eyes still had that flat look. "Is that what the sarge told you?"

"The sarge told me to decide for myself." Apparently Ryan didn't think the information was worth hiding anymore.

"Then do that," Clowes said. "Me, I don't have enough information. I want to find a body first, then wonder how he was killed."

"You don't think this blood's Dietl's?" Ryan asked.

"I don't think anything right now," Clowes said. "Let's just go."

He realized, after he spoke, that Ryan had probably been asking questions as a way to stall, not wanting to follow a trail like that to look for the body of a man who had shared more than one beer with them.

Ryan took a deep breath, and went to the right of the blood trail. Clowes went to the left. They moved slowly, constantly scanning everything ahead and behind. Clowes had that strange sense of being watched, but he saw nothing. There weren't even scavengers in the trees. No vultures, no insects, nothing except the flies on the tank, far behind them.

The shadows of the mesa had completely swallowed them by the time they reached the edge of the trees thirty paces away. The blood trail stopped abruptly. Clowes stopped too, beside the last tree, and sighed. How could a trail just end? Could this thing get any stranger?

Then he heard a faint buzzing. He raised his head. "Oh my God," Clowes said. "There he is."

Almost directly above hung Private Dietl's body. Or at least, it was someone's body. In the shadows it took Clowes a few seconds to understand exactly what he was looking at. The body was hanging from a rope tied around its feet. Every inch of skin had been peeled off, leaving muscles and intestines showing, now a reddish brown from the dried blood. The heart and lungs had been removed, and only the jawbone was left on the head. Something had removed the skull completely.

Clowes took a step back, almost tripping over a bush. His stomach wanted to pour out of his chest, and every muscle in his body was telling him to turn and run. Only his army training kept him from doing just that.

"I think I'm going to be sick," Ryan said softly as he too backed away from the grisly sight.

Hundreds of flies swarmed over the corpse, moving in and out of the chest cavity as if it were a hive. Clowes had skinned and hung his share of deer over the years. But he had no idea that a human could be skinned and hung too. There was one sick bastard running around out there, that much was for sure.

One sick, strong bastard. It had taken some work to kill Dietl like that, and even more to string him up from that tree.

Ryan choked, then coughed, but managed not to lose his dinner. Clowes moved over beside him, keeping his back on the body. "You all right?"

Ryan took a deep breath of the hot, evening air, then nodded.

Clowes did the same, ignoring the smell as best he could. And that damned feeling that they were not alone. It had to be a psychological reaction to the body. The trees were too far apart, and the scrub too small for anyone to hide here. A person could be seen a long distance off.

"Oh, man," Ryan said. "What are we going to do?"

"Report back to the sarge," Clowes said. "They got to get a team out here before there's nothing left of this body."

"Yeah," Ryan said, standing up straight and cradling his rifle in his arms. "Let's get the hell out of here."

Suddenly behind Ryan came a sound like a knife snapping open. The snick was accompanied by a cold, almost metallic sound that seemed to come out of thin air.

Ryan started to turn, but then the air shimmered and something huge and very sharp stabbed him in the back, lifting him off the ground like he was a child's toy. He didn't even have time to scream.

Hot blood splattered over Clowes, covering him. He instinctively dove backward and away, rolling in the dirt. He came up into a crouch, his rifle ready.

Ryan's body seemed to hang by itself in the air, held up by an unseen hand. He was clearly dead.

Clowes opened up, firing on full automatic, spraying Ryan with bullets, hoping to hit whatever was behind him. Ryan's body moved in a strange dance, limbs jerking as the bullets hit them.

The air shimmered behind Ryan, not once, but

twice, as Clowes's shots went through him. Clowes guessed that the shimmer meant the shots had hit their mark.

If there was something behind Ryan, it had to be getting pissed. And if Clowes were getting pissed, he would—

He saw the shimmer and had a half second to react. He dove to the right, rolling as a blue bolt of energy scored the ground where he had been an instant before.

Again he came up firing, spraying the air with a stream of bullets.

"Show yourself, you chickenshit!" he shouted.

Ryan's body dropped the ground. This time Clowes dove left, and was glad he did. Another blue streak had come out the thin air, exploding into the dirt where he had been.

This time he came up from his tumble running, heading for the nearest rocks. He needed some cover and he needed it quick.

He heard the crackling of the shot before he felt it tear through his back and explode out his chest. The force of the impact sent him flying forward. He tried to put his hands out to block his fall, but his arms didn't work anymore.

And in the seconds before his head smashed into the desert rock, he realized that he and Ryan were part of a hunt, but not the kind of hunt they had planned for their leave.

Clowes had never been prey before.

And he finally, in the last moment of his life, understood why prey usually lost.

6

My people are hunters. We have never been the hunted, except in the tale of the monster, told to us by our ancestors. Only the monster slayer, Nayenezgani, is a greater hunter than the monster. My brother is Nayenezgani, yet those who think they know all keep him from the monster. They have never heard the story of the monster slayer. Death awaits those who do not learn.

As it was most nights in the summer, the barracks had become an oven, heated by the blazing sun for fourteen hours. The breeze wasn't strong enough to bring in the cooler air of twilight. The open windows were taunting, promising more than they could give. By morning, though, the barracks would be freezing, the chilly desert night air making the place so cold that many of the guys waited until it was cool enough for blankets before falling asleep.

But no one was thinking of sleep yet. The mess had just finished serving dinner, and the evening hours stretched ahead, the only free time many of the soldiers would have all day. Most of them used it to write letters, read, or play cards. Others lined up at the phones inside the mess, hoping to talk to wives or girlfriends or family. And a few looked for trouble, but didn't find it. The base camp was too far out for that.

Corporal Nakai sat on his bunk, ignoring the heat, ignoring those who came and went around him. His thoughts were buried in the events of the morning. He went over every detail of Dietl's death, looking for anything that he could have done different. Maybe when he caught the odd smell, he should have insisted that they both crawl inside the tank. Maybe, if he could have kept Dietl from acting aggressively, it would have saved him.

But saved him from what? Whatever had killed Dietl could seem invisible in plain sight. It seemed to fire from out of nowhere. And its weapons were highly advanced.

The sound of gunfire echoed across the evening desert, bringing Nakai out of his thoughts. His grandfather's words rang through his mind.

Evil does not just go away. It must be defeated.

Nakai stood and headed toward the closest window. Private Kroft, wearing only his pants and T-shirt, leaned out another window, smoking, and staring out at the desert. His hairy arms bulged with muscle, and his neck was thick like a football player's. He took a long drag off the cigarette, clearly savoring the taste and the fact that it was against the rules. Nakai lived in the army, under more rules than he could remember. Breaking some of the small ones always felt good to him too. But the no-smoking rule was one that he liked. He hated the stench of tobacco. It dulled the senses, made the subtle scents disappear.

Right now Nakai didn't want any scents to disappear.

"You hear those shots?" Kroft asked as Nakai stopped at the window and looked off in the direction of the tank. In the fading light there wasn't much to see.

"Yeah," Nakai said.

More shots cut through the night air, then abruptly ceased. The quiet that followed seemed profound. Nakai strained to hear something else, anything else. But all he heard was Kroft inhaling, and a faint conversation behind him. The desert was silent.

Nakai didn't much like the silence. It meant something had ended. Remembering what had happened that morning, he doubted the silence was a good one. He just hoped the sarge had taken his advice and sent a dozen men out to investigate. If he sent only two or three, they were most certainly dead by now.

Nakai stepped back from the window. The air stank of cigarette smoke. His irritation flared. If he had been with Kroft this morning, neither of them would be alive now.

"Kroft," Nakai snapped, "get your head back in here and ditch that butt before the sarge comes by."

Kroft took a long, last drag off the cigarette, ground it out on the window ledge, and flicked the butt into the dirt.

Nakai sat down on his bunk, trying, without success, to keep the thoughts of this morning out of his mind. Those shots just now bothered him more than he wanted to admit.

"Hey, Nakai," Kroft said, turning from the window. His eyes glittered. Nakai recognized the look. Kroft was angry that Nakai had ordered him around. "Where the hell is Dietl? Is he still out there?"

Yeah. He was still out there. Nakai could still see that arc of energy appear in the empty sky and slice through Dietl's body. Dietl's eyes hadn't even widened with shock or surprise. He had died instantly.

And Nakai had left him in the desert with that thing.

He'd had no choice.

From two bunks down, Corporal Danken stood. Out of the corner of his eye Nakai watched him come. Danken was built like Kroft, with more muscle than brain. The two spent their off time together in the weight room. Nakai imagined that in school, both of them had been bullies. They hadn't changed much since.

Danken had black hair and fair skin pitted by dozens of acne scars. He was a good soldier, except for one fairly major problem: he hated all blacks and Native Americans. To him, anyone with dark skin was the enemy, tolerated only because of the rules.

"Yeah, where is Dietl?" Danken stopped next to Nakai's bunk.

Nakai ignored him. The sarge had ordered him to say nothing about Dietl. Nakai planned to follow that order, more for Dietl's sake than the sarge's.

Kroft pushed off the window ledge and stood. He reached for his cigarettes, then seemed to think the better of it. Or maybe he was trying, in a not-so-subtle way, to let Nakai know why the mood had shifted.

Kroft came up beside Danken. Now there were two muscle-bound idiots towering over Nakai. He suppressed a sigh. This was just what he didn't need. Not that it mattered. Even if he did say what happened to Dietl, no one would believe him. And even if they did believe him, that wouldn't stop them from looming over him. He had criticized Kroft, and Danken wouldn't stand for that. Danken used any excuse he could to turn on Nakai.

"Ah," Danken said, smiling at Nakai, "he's giving us his 'me strong, silent Navajo' act."

Kroft laughed, but Nakai kept his head down, staring at his pants.

"He ain't said a word," Danken said, "since we hauled in that funny-looking plane this afternoon."

Kroft left his thick arms fall to his sides. "Maybe," he said in a playful tone that implied he didn't believe a word he was about to say, "he's not supposed to talk. Maybe the sarge told him everything was top secret."

"You a Secret Agent Man, Nakai? Think you're James Bond?"

"Naw, he's Agent Smart."

"Got a phone in your shoe, Nakai?"

"In his heel," Kroft said.

Danken crossed his arms. Now the two men were standing in the exact same position. "You know, Nakai was alone, and he showed up after we found that plane."

"So?" Kroft asked.

"So, Dietl had nothing to do with the plane. So why can't he tell you where Dietl is?"

Nakai kept his head bowed, but he watched the two men out of the corner of his eye. It was becoming very clear they weren't going to go away without a little push. And if he was going to push, it might as well be with a clear message to leave him alone.

"Maybe he doesn't want to tell about Dietl," Kroft said. "Maybe he scalped him."

Nakai moved like a snake striking its prey. Quick, fast, and without warning. He came up off the bunk and planted his fist squarely on Kroft's chin, aiming the blow straight through to a spot beyond Kroft's thick head.

Kroft went down to the wood floor like a cement sack dropped from a truck. Nakai knew the blow hadn't broken anything, but the other man would be seeing stars for a time.

Danken's strong arms wrapped around Nakai, pinning him. "All right, Chief." Danken's voice sneered in Nakai's ear. "Let's see how you handle a real challenge."

Instantly, Nakai smashed his head backward in a snapping motion, connecting with Danken's nose. The crack echoed through the barracks.

Danken's grip loosened just enough for Nakai to break free. Then with a quick reverse kick, Nakai buried his foot squarely into Danken's stomach.

The breath left the corporal in a rush, spraying blood from the broken nose. Nakai stood, glancing around to see if anyone else wanted a part of the action. All the men in the barracks had surrounded the trio. They watched Nakai as if he were the dangerous one. He met their gazes one by one, challenging them. Most of the men looked away.

Kroft moaned and Nakai motioned for two privates to get him into his bunk. Danken was another matter. He was bleeding from his smashed nose, and having problems catching his breath. He'd be spending the night in the infirmary. And Nakai doubted that would improve his feelings toward people with dark skin.

"What the hell is going on in here?" Sarge's voice boomed through the barracks.

No one answered.

The sarge entered the room and walked to the circle of men. They parted to let him through. He stopped beside Danken, and put his hands on his hips.

"Looks like he took a nasty fall."

No one spoke. The other men didn't move. Nakai stayed in the center of the circle, and slowly, so that it wasn't noticeable, unclenched his fists.

Sarge pointed to two privates. "Help the corporal to the infirmary. Nakai, you come with me right now."

Nakai expected that. After all, he was the one still standing, and he had blood on his knuckles. His right fist throbbed from the force of his blow to Kroft's face. When the sarge turned his back, Nakai shook his fingers, trying to relax them. Nothing worked. He was going to have a sore hand for a day or so.

The sarge marched out of the barracks. Nakai followed.

The night was finally cool. The desert was silent. No more gunshots. No more anything. The light around the barracks was thin and artificial. Nakai could barely see the back of the sarge's head.

About ten steps away from the barracks, the sarge turned to face Nakai. "I don't suppose you want to tell me how that got started, do you?"

"I would rather not," Nakai said.

"As I figured," Sarge said, disgust in his voice. "Follow me."

Nakai had no idea where they were headed, but he suspected the sarge wasn't going to talk to him about the fight. He had a hunch the sarge wanted to talk to him about Dietl, the strange craft, and the gunfire that had ended only moments before.

7

It is difficult to know that I may help my brother only once, and then it must be in the fight with the monster. I must watch as he fights, picking my time. It is difficult. My desire is to help him in all things. But my brother is strong. He has never run from a fight, but he does not search out a fight. He has a balance far beyond his years. Our ancestors are pleased. As his brother, I am proud.

The sarge didn't say another word. He pivoted, and headed back toward the barracks.

The direction he walked in surprised Nakai. Nakai had been expecting the sarge to use the outside entrance to the officers' quarters. Instead, he headed toward the front hallway that connected Nakai's barracks to a half-dozen others along the base's main road. The sarge climbed the steps, and

Nakai followed, the sound of their boots on the wood echoing in the quiet night.

No more shooting.

No shouting.

The silence continued to grate on his nerves.

The sarge opened the double doors, and went inside. As Nakai stepped through the doors, he cringed. No one had opened windows in the hallway, and it was even hotter than his barracks had been. The usual odors of sweat and floor polish seemed stronger than normal. All the doors were closed, and the hallway was empty.

The sarge turned away from Nakai's barracks and headed toward "D" barracks at the far end of the hallway. The click of their boots on the smooth floor was the only sound.

"D" barracks was nearly empty, with most of its unit on maneuvers near Raton. The place felt abandoned. Nakai swallowed, wondering what the sarge had planned.

The sarge turned down a narrow hallway, and stopped halfway. He waited until Nakai caught up, then shoved open the nearest door, labeled STORAGE.

Nakai met the sarge's level gaze, unsure what was about to happen. The sarge hated him, Nakai knew that much. But not enough to lock him in a storage room in an empty barracks for fighting before lights-out. Something else was going on.

"Get in there," the sarge said, holding the door open.

Nakai didn't hesitate. He had no idea what the sarge had in mind, but he knew he could take him if he had to. The sarge was tough, but not that tough.

Inside the storage room only one lightbulb illuminated the space between boxes of toilet paper and a rack of brooms and shovels. The closet was hot, but not as hot as the hallway, and it too smelled of floor polish.

Nakai was all the way inside before he saw movement near the back of the closet. Colonel Athelry stepped forward as the sarge closed the door. Somehow that made the single bulb seem brighter. Athelry nodded to Nakai, then leaned back against some cases of bedding. He held two sheets of paper in his left hand, and even though he was staring at them, he didn't seem to be reading them. It seemed like this was a staged scene, especially for Nakai's benefit. Why, Nakai had no idea, but he'd bet he was about to find out. He snapped to attention, saluting.

"At ease," Colonel Athelry said. "Sorry I can't offer you a chair, son."

"I don't think the corporal minds, sir," the sarge said. Nakai turned slightly. He hadn't realized the sarge had come in with him.

Nakai stopped near the colonel and assumed the at-rest position. Nakai recognized the tone the colonel was using: friendly, wanting to impart bad news gently. This was not a good sign of what was about to come.

"Sorry to get you out so late, Corporal," the colonel said, "but as you can tell, we didn't want anyone to observe this meeting."

Nakai nodded.

The colonel stepped away from the crates. It was a signal that the friendliness was about to end. "Now, understand one thing, Corporal. This conversation goes no further than this storage closet. Whatever we tell you is *strictly classified.*"

"Yes, sir," Nakai said. He didn't add that there was no one he could tell, since Dietl, his only friend on the base, was dead.

The colonel nodded and glanced at the papers in his hand. "Preliminary testing on that ship we retrieved this morning has us worried." He paused for a moment, then looked Nakai right in the eye. "You were right. It most definitely is *not* a surveillance craft."

Nakai felt his breath catch in his throat. He swallowed before saying, "I was hoping I was wrong."

"So were we." The sarge had stopped beside Nakai and was also standing at rest.

"We believe," the colonel said, "that the ship is a hostile combat vessel, and we believe that you did indeed run into its operator."

Nakai felt his shoulders tighten. He didn't like how this was turning out. But then, he didn't know what they could tell him that would make things better.

"Were you able to retrieve Dietl's body?" he asked. His people never abandoned the dead. He knew he would have to live with that action for a long time to come.

The colonel glanced at Sarge. There was something in that look, a communication that confirmed Nakai's suspicions. The shots he had heard were the signs of a mission gone wrong.

"I'm afraid the retrieval team," the colonel said, "ran into some resistance. We have others going out now."

"Better make it a platoon," Nakai said. Then realizing that he nearly made a faux pas, he added, "Sir."

A shadow passed over the colonel's eyes. Apparently, he had already realized that—too late, of course.

The sarge cleared his throat, but the colonel didn't seem to take the hint. The loss of the retrieval team obviously disturbed him.

The sarge took a deep breath, and turned to Nakai. "The fact that this intruder got so close to the base poses some serious questions about our security."

Nakai hadn't even thought of that. He had been too concerned about Dietl, and the loss of the tank.

The sarge's words seemed to break the colonel's reverie. "Without his craft," the colonel said, "I doubt that he's much of a threat to the base as a whole."

Nakai nodded, but didn't believe the colonel for a moment. The fighter that had killed Dietl this morning would be a very serious threat to anyone. But it wasn't Nakai's place to argue with a colonel. He'd nearly made that mistake a moment ago.

"On the other hand," the colonel continued, glancing at the sarge, "the pilot of that craft is probably anxious to eliminate the only person who can recognize him."

Nakai felt his heart pump harder. So this was what they had brought him here for. This was the bad part, the reason the three of them were hiding in a storage closet.

"The sergeant and I have decided it's best that you take that leave from the base."

"Colonel," Nakai said, frowning. "The intruder is armed with—"

"I remember what you told me, son," the colonel said. "After we inspect Dietl's body, we should have a better idea of what we're up against."

"But, sir—" Nakai said.

The colonel held up his hand. "Son, your being here may also complicate matters for us. Trust our judgment on this one."

Nakai said nothing. He had been in the army long enough not to trust their judgment on anything. But he had also been in the army long enough to keep quiet about his lack of faith in the system.

"I've pushed through your three-day pass," the colonel said. "It will take effect tomorrow morning."

"We'll provide transportation to the nearest bus stop," the sarge said. "I know we can count on your confidentiality."

Nakai said nothing. The two other men looked at each other. Apparently they had thought a pass would make him happy. They probably thought this was the easiest way to silence him. He could almost hear the sarge recommending the plan: *Nakai'll be so pleased to go that he'll do anything we want. Hell, by the time he gets back, he'll probably have forgotten anything strange had happened.*

As if he could. But they hadn't been in that desert this morning. They hadn't known how close he had come to the same kind of instant death that had taken Dietl.

"Really," the colonel said, "this is for the best, for all involved. I'm sure you can see that."

Nakai said nothing. This was the best for them, of course. But it probably was not the best for all involved. In fact, he couldn't think of a worse plan. He was the only one who knew how the intruder operated, what kind of weaponry it had—at least, he could guess that it was more sophisticated than the army's, judging by those blue bolts—and he knew how quick it was. The corporal and the sarge had asked perfunctory questions this morning, but they hadn't believed him. And now they were sending him away.

"You can see that, can't you, Corporal?" the sarge asked. "That this is for the best?"

They wanted him to answer. They needed his verbal agreement. His silence was bothering them, just as it had bothered Danken.

"Yes, sir," Nakai said, not wanting to get into any more trouble. He could speak up, of course, but it would do no good. They had already devised a plan. They had already made up their minds about this intruder, and they had already figured out a way to handle the problem.

So what if it didn't work.

"Good, Corporal. I'm glad you understand," the colonel said. He nodded to the sarge, then turned his attention back to Nakai. "You are dismissed."

Nakai saluted, then spun and left Sergeant Coates and Colonel Athelry in the storage closet. He had to get out of there quickly before he lost all control and told them how stupid he thought their plan was. His best—his *only*—friend had died this morning, and instead of letting Nakai help them get vengeance for that death, they were making him leave. He would have been an asset to them, but they didn't see it that way.

They saw him as trouble. They had always seen him as trouble. And, like always, they were wrong.

At a quick walk, he headed for the mess hall. He had a phone call to make before he tried to sleep. Alda was going to be surprised, and happy he was coming, even though, at the moment, he wasn't.

8

It was said by our ancestors that the monster would come on the wings of death. Because the saying was in a song, for a long time my people thought it spoke of the past. We know now that it spoke of the future. Many things were not understood by my people. It was not understood by my grandfather, and those who came before him, just how much death one monster could bring. If it could not be understood by our people, it could not be understood by those who kept my brother from that which he was supposed to slay.

Under the darkness of the New Mexico sky, the night seemed like any other. The wild boar were snuffling in the dirt a mile from their previous hunting ground. The great cat that had hunted them the night before did not watch them this night. The death of the boar had reminded it that two-legged hunters sometimes killed cats, and it had decided to give that particular hunting ground a rest. It would return when the time felt right.

In a small copse of trees not far from the base, another hunter considered his prey. The hunter carried three skulls already, human skulls, and one tiny boar skull hung from his belt. He tapped his long nails on a metal device he wore on his powerful left forearm. The time was not right yet.

He would wait until it was.

Several miles away, in the yard of that base, Corporal Benson sat in a running humvee. The cool of the night air felt good. He liked New Mexico best in the dark. He was from Maine, and even though he had been stationed here for more than a year, the excessive heat still seemed unnatural to him. The only times he was comfortable were times like this. In the cool darkness. He often volunteered for pre-dawn duty. It was quarter of five in the morning, and the sun wasn't yet a hint in the eastern sky. The longer it stayed away, the happier he would be. The stars poked through the night-lights of the base perimeter, invading the sky above with faint reminders of how beautiful a night sky could be.

He stretched and wondered if he would be able to stay awake, even with the humvee rattling beneath him. The vehicle had a rough idle, and when he got the chance, he would take a look at it himself. He had already complained to the grease monkeys and they had looked at him as if he hadn't known a thing about military equipment. Maybe he didn't, but he knew something about cars. And this one, no matter what its designation, needed a little work under the hood.

Maybe he would start that work now. He had

been sitting here long enough, and it would serve the corporal right to be forced to wait. Benson had to do something to remain alert. He'd managed only about two hours of sleep last night, due to a poker game in the barracks laundry room. The game was going his way, as it usually did among the amateurs here, but when he finally noticed the time, around one A.M., he realized he still needed to lose a few small hands before he left. He didn't want the boys to figure out too soon that he knew more about cards than they did. So he played for another forty-five minutes, carefully giving back one percent of his take. Then he stood and made a show of being disappointed with the turn in his luck before heading off to bed. But he really hadn't thought the day through. Now, with this transport duty followed by his new assignment of helping out in the hangar after breakfast, he was going to pay the price.

At least he was richer this morning than he had been at this time yesterday.

Benson stretched again, and then saw movement to the left. Corporal Nakai closed the barracks door behind him and headed down between the white stones that marked the front walk of "C" barracks. He was carrying a heavy duffel over his shoulder, and he did not look happy. Most men ran to the humvee when they were granted leave. Benson should know. He been assigned to the car pool for months, and had the unenviable job of shuttling anyone with a higher rank in and out of the small nearby town, at no matter what time of day or night. He was getting used to that rap on the door that signaled a new assignment. Fortunately, he had gotten this one before lights-out. If it had come in the middle of the night, he would have been hard-pressed to explain his absence from his bunk.

This assignment was strange, though. It was well known that the sarge hated Nakai, and did everything he could to make the man's life miserable. That Nakai got a sudden leave, and that Benson was assigned to drive him, was just plain weird. Nakai was being treated like a man of higher rank, like someone important. If Benson had had to bet that someone in the barracks would get the royal treatment, he wouldn't have laid his money on Nakai.

Nakai tossed his duffel in the back of the open humvee and slid into the passenger seat. He was a big man who looked smaller until you sat close to him. He also had a quiet power that Benson respected.

But that respect didn't stop him from giving Nakai a hard time. "I thought you were going to be here fifteen minutes ago."

Nakai pulled his jacket closer. "Thought you liked the early-morning cold. Figured you'd want a little time to bond with it."

"I thought you had a bus to catch."

"The 5:07 to La Barca de Oro. We still have time, don't we?"

Of course they did, and Nakai knew it. Benson had a reputation for taking the humvees out full throttle, especially this early, when no one else was on the roads.

"I'll see what I can do," Benson said. He swung the humvee around and headed for the main gate. "You know, you could have taken a later bus."

"You ever ridden a bus in the summer heat?" Nakai asked.

"Gotcha." Benson hadn't ridden a bus in desert heat, and the thought made him sweat just thinking about it, even with the chilly night air around them. Maybe it *had* been Nakai's choice to leave this early. Then again, maybe not.

The scuttlebutt last night at the game had Corporal Nakai leaving a post, and running into the pilot of the weird craft now stored in the hangar. One of the guys had said the colonel wanted to get rid of Nakai until everything calmed down. And shipping him out this early certainly seemed to be confirmation of that rumor.

The front-gate guards waved them by without much more than a pause. As Benson ground the vehicle up to speed, he glanced at Nakai. "Weird how the colonel suddenly okayed your pass, isn't it?"

Nakai never took his gaze off the road ahead. "Yeah. Weird."

He spoke in a flat monotone that led Benson to believe that he didn't think it weird at all.

"What're you going to do?"

Nakai shrugged. "The usual."

The humvee bumped over the rutted road. Benson held the steering wheel tightly, then glanced at Nakai. Nakai's face seemed purposely blank.

"Something happen yesterday?"

"Why?"

"I've been hearing strange rumors."

"There're always strange rumors," Nakai said, looking out at the scrub. He pulled his cap over his face, slumped in the seat, and didn't say another word. Benson didn't force the issue. Nakai seemed unusually tense. He wasn't sleeping, despite his posture. He was studying the dark desert on both sides of the road as if he were watching for something. Benson kept his eyes glued to the pavement in front of him and let the cool night air shove back some of the sleepless hours.

After a while he kicked the humvee to high speed, and enjoyed the breeze in his face. Nothing like the hours before dawn. Nothing like it at all.

The small town was still asleep when Benson swung through the main street. It looked like most northern New Mexico small towns, square squat buildings parked in the middle of the desert. Some, like Española, were surrounded by trees and spectacular mesas. Most were like this one, so poor that they didn't even bother to try to hide it.

Benson pulled in front of the fake adobe building with a Greyhound sign tacked to the grimy window. Nakai swung out of the vehicle, grabbed his duffel, and slung it over his shoulder.

"Thanks," he said.

Benson didn't know if Nakai was thanking him for the ride or for not asking questions. He suspected it was both. "See ya in a few days."

"I hope so," Nakai said as he turned and walked away.

Benson had no idea what these words meant, but he wasn't about to ask. He shrugged and swung the humvee around. If he hurried, he'd have time for breakfast. And, God knew, he needed the coffee.

An hour later, when Benson entered the hangar, the sight of the captured craft stopped him cold. He had seen it yesterday, but its strangeness hadn't really registered. Now, seeing it sitting on the back of the flatbed truck, he was shocked. It didn't look man-made at all. Sitting in the rocks, it had almost blended in. Here in the hangar, it just looked alien.

Its lines and angles were unusual. Where he expected sharp corners, there were curves. Where he expected curves, there were sharp corners. Red lights—at least he thought they were lights—up front were angled like the eyes of a Siamese cat. And instead of one light on each side, there were two.

In the top center of the nose, rounded metal rose, almost like hubcaps stuck on the nose for decoration. The craft wasn't yellow, wasn't orange, wasn't gold or brown, but it was a combination of the colors, all of them at the same time. It depended on where he stood and how he stood, and the way the light hit the sides.

And those sides. He wasn't sure if they were made of metal or not—they looked like they were—but not of any metal he had ever seen.

He had been gaping. He knew it. Fortunately no one else seemed to notice. No one except the sentry who stood at the hangar's bay door. He grinned and winked as Benson shook himself. Apparently the sentries, at least, had had the same reaction.

There were two other sentries standing before the doors of the hangar. Benson wondered why they were inside. He had noted guards on the outside as well.

Next to the inside sentries, three men in white lab coats were setting up equipment. One man stood at a table on which there was a very sophisticated laptop computer. The screen was covered with a series of orange numbers that made no sense to Benson.

With one more glance at the guard, Benson

climbed up on the back of the truck and took up his assigned position on the lift. This much of his duty had already been explained to him. He was to help hoist the craft off the flatbed and into a specially prepared area of the hangar. Around the hangar, activity was starting to increase. From his perch he could see most of it. And since he didn't have anything to do until they decided to move the craft, he could just sit and watch.

Two of the white-lab-coat guys were studying the ship, moving around it slowly, making notes as they went. Another crew was working to set up the area where the ship would be placed, installing more machines and checking video equipment.

The conversations were muted, but the hangar was so large that the sounds echoed and played back, almost like reverb at a stadium rock concert. Suddenly, silence fell over the hangar as Colonel Athelry entered, followed closely by Sergeant Coates. Athelry looked tired. Even his mustache was drooping. Coates's normally red face was even redder. Both men stopped and gaped at the alien craft, just as Benson had. He shot another glance at the guard. The guard grinned.

Then the colonel shook himself, and elbowed the sergeant, who looked like he was coming out of a dream. They strode over to a spot below Benson, where a man in a white coat stood.

"Morning, Dr. Richards," the colonel said.

"Morning, sir," Richards said.

Around the hangar the activity went back to normal, but the colonel and the doctor remained close enough for Benson to hear.

The doctor was far from a typical military type.

He wore thick glasses, was mostly bald, and was un-naturally thin except for a bowling-ball-sized belly that made him look suspiciously like a python that had just eaten a meal. Benson hadn't seen the doc-tor around the base before. He must have flown in yesterday after the craft had been found.

"Any new developments yet, Doctor?" the colo-nel asked.

"It's clearly a spacecraft of some sort or an-other," Dr. Richards said, handing the colonel a clip-board covered with papers. "But almost all the radioactivity indicating deep-space travel has dissi-pated. Quite fascinating, actually."

"I'm sure it is, Doctor," the colonel said, glanc-ing through the papers the doctor had handed him. "But I'm more concerned at the moment with the questions Washington's going to be asking, such as where did it come from, is it alone, and are we in danger?"

"Has the pilot realized that we have his craft?" Sergeant Coates said.

"That also," the colonel said.

Benson made himself swallow and forced him-self to keep his eyes on the controls of his lift. The air was caught in his throat. He was sitting next to a radioactive alien spacecraft. What the hell were they doing to him?

He almost jumped down from the lift, then managed to calm his nerves. The doctor had said the radioactivity had faded. Clearly, since the colonel and the doctor were standing closer to the craft than he was, he would be all right.

With another deep breath he felt himself relax a little more. He was going to have to be calm when he worked the lift, that much was for sure. They didn't need him dropping the alien ship.

Below him the colonel kept studying the papers the doctor had handed him. Benson had no idea if the colonel and Sarge knew he could hear them, but he was sure he wasn't *supposed* to be hearing them. Especially if they thought this might be an alien craft. God, he'd heard about this crap before, but that's what he thought it was—crap. He'd seen the fake TV shows about extraterrestrials, and he'd decided that people were gullible enough to fall for anything.

Until now.

The ship glimmered in the light. He squinted at the sides. He was right: it was not yellow, orange, gold, or brown. It was a color he'd never seen before. One he couldn't even describe. A shiver ran through him, and he swallowed hard. This whole thing unnerved him.

Just as the colonel finished reading, a side door of the hangar opened and Sergeant Redman stepped in at a fast walk. Redman had been Benson's sergeant for almost six months. He was a good, but strict, sarge. Benson preferred him to Coates.

Redman was dressed in full battle gear and had his rifle slung over his shoulder. He looked more worried than Benson had ever seen him.

Redman hesitated slightly when he saw the alien craft, then went right up to the colonel and saluted. "Sir, we found Dietl, Lee, and Clowes." He hesitated a moment, then said, "All dead, sir."

Benson cursed softly to himself. He had liked Clowes. Liked him a lot, actually. He had played a lot of hands of poker against Clowes. The guy had been good.

The colonel turned. He didn't even look surprised. Benson felt his own chill grow. The colonel had already known they were dead. But how?

"What took so long to find them?" he asked.

Sergeant Redman took a deep breath, then glanced up at the alien craft before going on. "All three were hung from the trees near the tank placement. They were skinned, sir."

"Skinned?" Sergeant Coates asked.

"Skinned," Redman answered. "And their heads are missing. It's not a pretty sight."

Benson swallowed hard. Jesus. What had he gotten in the middle of?

"Have you secured the area?" the colonel asked.

"We have," Redman said. "But the men are jumpy, sir. Real jumpy."

"We all are," the colonel said. "Keep the area under wraps and get the med boys out there."

"Yes, sir," Redman said, saluted and left.

"Holy shit," Sergeant Coates said, more to himself than anyone else. Benson couldn't have agreed more.

The colonel took a deep breath, then turned to Dr. Richards. "I need answers and I need them quickly."

"We're doing our best," the doctor said. He appeared to be the only one who was calm.

Of course he would be. He hadn't known any of the men. Benson had known them all. He was shaking and his palms were damp. Damn. He wished he had found a way to get out of this duty. He was beginning to envy Nakai. He would have loved a three-day leave. This seemed like a good place to get out of.

"Doctor!"

The shout interrupted the conversation. Benson glanced down on the other side of the alien craft. One of the other men in a white coat was yelling for the doctor to come look at something. This one was a short guy, with black hair and no chin. And right at the moment he seemed as excited as if he had just won the lottery.

The doctor, colonel, and the two sergeants all moved around to the other side of the alien craft.

"Doctor," the short guy said. "We've got activity from the ship." He pointed up to a row of lights.

From Benson's position on top of the lift, he could see that red lights had appeared on the side and top of the alien craft. A row of them, blinking. Benson was sure they hadn't been there just a minute before.

As Benson watched, one of the red lights on the end of the row stopped blinking and went dark. The row got shorter.

Then a moment later another light went out. There were only six blinking red lights left.

The line of red lights was getting shorter and shorter. Suddenly Benson knew what was happening and what those red lights meant.

"I don't like the looks of this," the doctor said.

Benson couldn't help himself anymore. He leaned over the lift controls and yelled. "It looks like a countdown."

Five red lights were left.

The sarge looked up and frowned at him, but at that moment Benson didn't care in the slightest. He

didn't want to be sitting on top of the stupid lift
when that last red light went out. He swung off the
lift and scrambled down.

Four red lights left.

"I think the corporal is right," the doctor said.
"It does appear to be a countdown."

Three red lights blinked their warning.

Benson hit the floor of the hangar and took off
running.

Behind him the colonel shouted, "Everyone get
down!"

Two red lights.

Around Benson, men scrambled for cover. Benson dove in behind a large truck and rolled to a position behind a tire.

One red light blinked on the side of the alien
ship. One small red light.

And then it too went out.

There was a click. A very loud click that echoed
through the large hangar.

And that click was the last thing anyone in that
hangar heard. Within a fraction of a second, the entire base was wiped off the face of the planet.

Corporal Benson, Sergeant Coates, Colonel
Athelry, and the other thousand or so men and
women stationed in the New Mexico desert didn't
even know what hit them. They died instantly,
vaporized into a gray dust that over the years would
scatter across the desert and mix with the red sand
and dirt.

In a tree three miles away, the hunter watched
the dust cloud rise to the sky.

Forty miles away, on an old Greyhound bus
thirty minutes short of its destination, Corporal

Nakai dozed, his head banging slightly against the dirty glass. His dreams were of the hunt.

His dreams were of his grandfather.

His dreams were of a dead brother he didn't even know.

9

A warrior's place is in battle. A hunter's place is in the hunt. Take the hunter from the hunt and he loses his way. A man who loses his way turns inside. And sometimes the things inside are as threatening as the things outside. My brother left the monster behind, so my brother had to face another foe. A very old foe who had defeated our father. It is the way of the hunter.

Ben's Saloon was tucked on a dusty corner of the small town of Agate, New Mexico. Nestled almost exactly halfway between two reservations, Agate was the only place to get a stiff drink within fifty miles, and Ben's Saloon was the only place in Agate that served liquor.

Even on the brightest of days, no sunlight penetrated Ben's dim, smoky interior, and people entering during the afternoon always stood for a moment just inside the door to let their eyes adjust. The place had a run-down feel, as if the saloon was as tired as the land that surrounded it. Old beer signs over the bar were coated with a layer of dust, their plastic chipped and faded. Beer glasses covered the back bar in front of two large mirrors. A crack ran up one side of the right mirror, the remains of a forgotten bar fight.

The long, wooden bar was the saloon's most striking feature. It ran for almost forty feet and had been polished to a shine by Ben, the rail-thin owner. If he wasn't pouring a drink, he was polishing the bar. He kept the bar so polished that on a slow night he could slide a full glass of beer the entire length without spilling a drop.

The floor was made of boards that had cracked and settled over time. Even a sober man would stagger a bit as he crossed Ben's floor. A jukebox sat near the door. A dozen wooden tables and fifty or so chairs filled the main area. Each table had two ashtrays in the center and nothing more. The surface of each was scarred with the nicks and scratches of time; a few had names carved into the wood. Most were faded, the stain long gone.

Two bar-sized pool tables filled the back corner of the room, their green felt almost white in places from use. Dozens of cigarette burns dotted the rails and the felt had been patched on both tables. One table stood in a dip in the floor, and the regulars knew the right moment to brush against the table's side so that a shot did or didn't go into the hole.

Ben's did a tremendous business on the weekend. Its business midweek was also good—in the early evening. But by one in the morning, only a few dozen regulars usually remained. This night was no different.

Most of the regulars sat along the bar. However, two played pool, and judging by their looks of concentration—and the fact that they were playing on the table that didn't move—the stakes were high. Ben knew all of his regulars by their first names and considered many his closest friends, because he spent most every night with them. He even knew the names of the former regulars. And the former regular who sat alone at a table against the wall was one that Ben had hoped would never return to this bar. Not because Ben didn't like him, but because he did.

Corporal Enoch Nakai had put his life together in the last few years, but when he walked into the bar about twelve hours ago, Ben wondered if that fragile stability would hold. By the time Nakai asked for his third Jack Daniel's, Ben knew that it wouldn't. At three, tired of refilling Nakai's glass, he had let him keep the bottle. It had been full then. Now, ten hours later, it was mostly gone.

What Ben didn't know was what had pushed Nakai to this place. And it was a combination of factors. It was the feeling of helplessness that Nakai couldn't shake. It was the orders to leave when something inside him told him he needed to stay. And it was that image of his friend Dietl, in his last moment of life, a blue blade of energy cutting him in half.

Ben didn't know and didn't ask. He didn't believe in bartender-as-father-confessor. But he was relieved when the doors opened and a striking young woman entered. She wore a red shirt and jeans. Her long black hair was pulled back into two braids and she had on stained tennis shoes. She was one of his regulars. She was also the person he needed to see right then.

"Hi, Alda," Ben said. "Just get off work?"

"About five minutes ago," she said.

Alda worked days at Cindy's Hotel and Restaurant, the only place to stay and get a good meal in Agate. She was the main waitress and cleaning person—basically, Cindy's right hand. Everyone knew that she and Nakai were a couple, and most times no one bothered her, even though Nakai was away in the army.

She glanced over at Nakai and then gave Ben a questioning look. Ben felt a surge of guilt, as if it were his fault that Nakai had the bottle before him. But if Ben took charge of every alcoholic who came into the place, he wouldn't have any business at all.

"He hasn't caused any problems," Ben said, deliberately misunderstanding her look. "But he ain't up for driving."

The disappointment in her dark eyes was eloquent. She had been waiting two months to see Nakai, only to have him show up and hit the bottle. She looked reluctant to walk over to him, so Ben asked her the question he'd been asking everyone else all day: "Say, you hear anything more about that explosion this morning?"

A few of the regulars along the bar turned their attention to Ben's question. Agate, New Mexico, had been rocked early this morning, followed shortly by a rolling boom of thunder.

"We ain't heard a word in here," one of the regulars added, knowing Alda sometimes got news at Cindy's that didn't make it to the bar.

Alda moved up to the edge of the polished bar. "I heard nothing at all. A lot of people asked about it, though."

"Must have been a big one, to shake the ground like that," Ben said. A couple of the regulars agreed.

"Who knows what kind of tests they are doing down there at the base?" the same regular said.

Alda shot a sad glance at Nakai. "Sometimes I really don't want to know."

"Yeah," Ben said, "I asked your boyfriend there if he knew anything and he just gave me the cold stare."

Alda nodded. "He does that at times."

Ben laughed. "He could have just said he didn't know."

"Not Enoch," Alda said, smiling and glancing over at her drunken boyfriend. "That's not like him at all."

She wasn't just referring to his silence. He had been so proud of his sobriety, and he had vowed never to fall off the wagon. He had nearly lost everything before. He hadn't wanted to lose again.

"I suppose you're right," Ben said, although he knew a million drunks who had made the same vow, and somehow ended back up perched on their favorite stool. "You need help getting him home?"

"I don't think so," Alda said. "He's a pretty tame drunk."

"I remember," Ben said. "Wonder what kicked him off the wagon?"

Alda shook her head. "Something did. And after what happened to Enoch's father, it had to be something major, that's for sure."

Ben didn't know the story of Nakai's father, although Alda had alluded to it before. It was another thing he didn't want to know.

"Well," he said, polishing the bar in front of him, even though it really didn't need it. "Holler if you need help."

"Thanks," Alda said.

He watched her walk over to Nakai and wondered what the attraction was. Sure, Nakai was a good-looking man. But he never said much, and he rarely smiled. Ben wished he could hear the conversation now, then decided he didn't want to. He clicked on the radio beneath the bar, hoping for news.

Alda took her time getting to Nakai's table. He didn't notice her coming. When she reached his favorite spot, she leaned down beside him and said, "You about ready to head home?"

"With you?" he asked, his words slurring.

"With me." She reached out her hand to help him stand. How many times had they played this game? She didn't know. All she knew was that she had thought the game long over.

Nakai shook off her offer of help. He used the table for leverage, pushed too hard, and went right over backward, ending up in a tangled heap with the chair on the wood floor.

Alda just shook her head in disgust, then glanced over at Ben and the regulars watching along the bar. "Guess I'm going to need some help with the army boy here."

Ben laughed.

Nakai slept, his legs tangled in the chair, his mind finally clear of the images of Dietl. And of the fear of what was to come.

10

My brother did not win the fight with the demon that killed our father. He did not even fight this night, but instead gave himself willingly to the enemy. I fear my brother may not be strong enough to win the fight against the monster who now walks among the people.

The morning dawned bright and clear over the reservation outside of Agate, New Mexico. The sky had a faint reddish tint to it that the old-timers said was blood filling the day.

This morning, they were right, but no one knew it yet. The children had just finished their chores and headed off in groups to play before the heat drove them inside. Those men with jobs were already at work. The farmers and ranchers were tending to their lands. So far, it seemed like another normal day.

Down the old highway to the west of the reservation, a dozen small farms clung to the desert like
flies to the back of a dead horse. The houses were
not much more than faded wood shacks, the yards a
patchwork of weeds, old cars, and rusting farm
equipment. A new Ford pickup turned in to one of
the driveways and kicked up a small cloud of dust as
it stopped. Dan Bonney climbed out, stuck a cigarette in the side of his mouth, and paused to light it.
He took a long puff, felt the nicotine catch and hold,
and then he went to the back of the truck. The cigarette was an important part of his work. Much as he
loved the job, he hated the stink that surrounded
live animals.

Dan Bonney was a shearer and wool buyer for
three firms down in Albuquerque. Part of his terri-
tory was the reservations of northern Arizona and
New Mexico. Most people assumed he was an ath-
lete, probably a basketball player. He stood well over
six feet tall, and had a graceful athletic build. His
arms were corded with muscle. But he got paid for
his abilities with sheep, not his abilities on a basketball court. He could shear a sheep in less than a minute, and was known in the area for being fair with
his prices. Almost everyone liked him.

Dan grabbed a bunch of tools from the bed of
the truck and headed around the side of the shack.
As he did, the farmer came outside. Robert Nadire
was a weathered man in his fifties. Dan had known
him for years. Robert's family had lived and worked
the surrounding land as sheep herders for three generations. He had almost a hundred sheep in the hills
nearby and was making just enough off of their wool

and meat to get by. Last night he had brought in twelve to be sheared.

"Morning, Dan," Robert said, pulling back his long black hair to get it out of the faint breeze. Beside him a young boy of six, his youngest son, stayed near the door, as if afraid. Dan smiled at the kid, but the smile didn't break the fear. Nothing did. That boy had been afraid of Dan from the first time they met, when the kid was still in diapers. Robert's wife had watched the interaction, over five years ago now, and said, "It's almost as if he sees death behind you."

"Hey, Robert," Dan said, dropping his equipment beside the sheep pen. "You forget how to count?"

"No." Robert sounded a bit offended.

"I thought you said twelve," Dan said.

Robert walked up to the sheep pen and peered inside. He frowned as if he couldn't believe what he was seeing. He quickly checked the gate, but it was latched. "There were twelve here last night."

The boy swallowed hard and pressed himself against the door. He was staring at Dan as if Dan were at fault.

Dan suppressed a sigh. He'd seen this happen before. He took a good look at the dirt near the pen. He didn't notice anything unusual, but then tracking wasn't his specialty. "Maybe one of the big cats got them."

The population of puma in the area had been increasing over the last few years, and the sheep ranchers were feeling the pressure the worst. But the state protected the big cats and there wasn't a hell of a lot any of the farmers could do about them.

Dan shoved his hands in his pockets. The sheep were acting more skittish than usual this morning. They were huddled on the far side of the pen, as if they were trying to hide. That was unusual in and of itself. Sheep deserved their reputation as some of nature's most stupid animals. They didn't have enough of a memory to recognize Dan from his semiannual visits.

"I don't see how a cat could have gotten in," Robert said, moving along the pen between the fence and the house. "I would have heard, and there would be signs that—"

He stopped abruptly, head down. Dan glanced at the boy, who was still watching them, eyes wide. The kid gave him the creeps.

Dan shook off the feeling and walked over to Robert. Robert was staring at the ground before him.

A large pool of blood, some of it still red and fresh, filled the area between the house and the pen. Red and fresh. That meant that whatever had taken the sheep was still here, or newly gone. Had the truck scared the creature off?

Most likely. But what kind of cat attacked a ranch in broad daylight?

Then Dan heard a splash. The pool of blood rippled. Simultaneously, he and Robert looked up. The blood was dripping from the roof of the shack. But how was that possible? Predators in this part of the country didn't carry their prey *upward*. They dragged an injured or dead animal to a private spot in the desert and feasted.

This behavior was unusual enough to make him very nervous.

Dan moved back around the pen and indicated

that Robert should step away from the building with him. Robert held out a hand to his son so that the boy wouldn't move. Not that he was going to. The kid looked like he was glued to the shack's front door.

When Dan and Robert had both gone a few feet, Dan turned around and saw a sight that chilled him down to his bones.

On the roof were the remains of the two sheep. From the looks of it, they had been gutted and their heads cut off. Most of the wool was stained red, and one of the sheep looked to be half-eaten.

"How in the hell did they get up there?" Robert asked.

Dan didn't answer. He couldn't. He watched as some unseen force ripped the remaining sheep in half. He couldn't see what had done it, and that made the hair on the back of his neck rise.

"Son," Dan said to the young boy standing on the porch, "go fetch your father's rifle."

The young boy nodded. His eyes grew wider, if that were possible. Dan was about to issue the order again when a blue flash appeared above the bodies of the sheep on the roof. Like a bolt of lightning it shot out and stuck Robert square in the chest, exploding blood and intestines all over the fence.

"What the—?"

But before Dan could say another word, another bolt struck him, severing his head as if it had never really been attached.

And the little boy watched, frozen in place, as the vision he had seen for as long as he could remember came true.

11

My brother sleeps the sleep of the dead. He has lost a battle with the demon that killed our father, but he has not yet lost the war. For the moment that fight must wait. The monster walks in blood and my brother is Nayenezgani, the monster slayer. He must prepare for the fight. He cannot hide as our father did. He must face his demons. He will not listen to me. He does not know me. But he knows our grandfather, remembers and loves him, and still misses him. Our grandfather will visit him in his dreams and warn him.

Nakai let the booze wipe his memory clean. He didn't know that Alda and Ben had gotten him to his feet and dragged him to Alda's car. He didn't know that she had struggled with his weight after they reached her house, and that for a long moment she thought of leaving him sprawled in the backseat. Finally, though, she'd gotten him inside, and into bed.

And there his oblivion continued. Until a dream invaded his mind. If he were conscious, that would have been how he thought of it. But he wasn't. His abilities to reason had been short-circuited by the booze. So he couldn't block the dream.

He could only feel it.

And the dream feels odd because the sky is swirling green, the desert sand blue, the rocks black.

Nakai sits, his back against a rock, his feet outstretched, a bottle of bourbon in his hand. He is sixteen and has stolen the bottle. He is about to take another drink when his grandfather appears in front of him, shimmering into being like a mirage on a hot desert road.

Before Nakai can speak, his grandfather knocks the bottle from his hands, spilling the bourbon into the dirt and sand. The bourbon runs out, turning the dirt bloodred. The liquid grows into a puddle, then into a pool, growing larger and larger, as if it were trying to become a spring of blood.

Nakai's grandfather is the medicine man for the tribe. He wears a battered cowboy hat, a blue vest, and three necklaces of stones around his neck. From one necklace hangs a hawk's claw.

"There will be no drinking so long as you live under my roof." Nakai's grandfather's voice sounds like thunder, filling the dream with dread.

Suddenly the ground shakes. All around Nakai there is red, blood is flowing in the dry streams, the sky is dripping blood. Nakai glances down at his army uniform, afraid it is being stained. But somehow the blood is running off it, swirling around his boots, covering the sand.

His grandfather now stands between two others, holding an umbrella over his head to protect all three from the rain of blood. On Grandfather's left is Nakai's mother, on the right is Nakai's father. They are wearing their wedding clothes, looking just as they did in the picture his grandfather keeps over the fireplace.

Nakai's father has a bottle of bourbon in his hand, but his grandfather doesn't seem to notice.

"How did you get here?" Nakai asks.

"I live here," his grandfather says.

"But—"

"*You* are the visitor here, Enoch," his grandfather says.

"Why am I here?"

"Because I brought you here," his grandfather says.

"Why?"

"To warn you," his grandfather says.

"Need a drink, son?" Nakai's father asks. He leers, the smile of a skeleton.

"I do not need to drink," Nakai says.

"Good," another voice says from Nakai's left.

Nakai turns, staring at a white figure without a face, without a body, only an outline against the bloodred rain.

"Who are you?" he asks, but somehow he senses the answer.

"I am your brother," the white shape says.

"But you're dead."

"I am," the brother said. "But I have never left you."

"How can I see you?" Nakai asks.

"In dreams," the white shape says, "anything is possible. Listen to our grandfather."

Nakai takes a step toward the white shape, but slips in the blood and falls, covering himself in red clay and mud.

Nakai's father laughs and takes a drink.

Nakai's mother says nothing.

Nakai's grandfather says, "You must stand against the blood. Allow your brother to stand with you."

Nakai fights to get up, only to slip over and over as his father laughs. Nakai finally stops trying, and all of them fade. The rain continues, turning into a downpour. Sheets of blood fall from the sky.

"No!" Nakai shouts. *"No!"*

But the more he shouts, the more he twists and turns in the hot blood, the more mired he becomes. He is unable to stand, unable to think, and all he wants is a drink—

"Nakai," a voice said, distant, yet familiar. "Wake up. You're having a nightmare."

The blood faded. The tangle around his legs was caused by bedclothes, not by mud. Light poured in from a nearby window.

Sunlight. He had never been so happy to see it in his life.

Alda sat beside him on the bed, her hand on his shoulder, soothing him.

Nakai stared at her for a moment, afraid to close his eyes for fear the dream would return. It had been a long time since he had dreamed like that. It had felt so real he was afraid the sheets were covered in the blood. But they were only damp with his sweat.

Alda held out her hand. "Here, take these." She shoved two white pills into his hand, then took a glass of water off the nightstand and handed it to him.

He looked at the pills for a moment, the images of blood still filling his mind.

"Aspirin," Alda said. "After that much drinking, you're going to need aspirin and lots of water."

She was right. Some of his disorientation was coming from a hell of a hangover.

He managed to push the two pills into his mouth and with a shaking hand got the water to wash them past his parched throat. He handed the glass back to her. "Thanks."

He managed to rub a little of the grit out of his eyes and the dream faded a little, but not much. "What a weird dream."

Alda stopped near the foot of the bed, holding the glass of water. For the first time Nakai noticed she was completely dressed, wearing a red flannel shirt and jeans. Her long black hair was loose around her head, draping over her shoulders like a thick blanket.

"Seemed like more of a nightmare," Alda said, "judging by the way you were thrashing around."

"Yeah," Nakai said. "I suppose it was. My grandfather, my parents, and my brother were all in it."

"Your brother and mother?" Alda said. "I thought your twin brother was stillborn and your mother died during his birth."

"Yeah," Nakai said, still seeing the blood everywhere around him, tainting the entire room. He'd been hungover before, but never like this. And never with such a clear memory of a dream.

Slowly, making sure the room wasn't spinning too badly, he pushed himself up into a sitting position on the side of the bed. His undershirt was stained with sweat and he had no memory at all of getting into bed the previous night. The drinking had at least dulled the memory of seeing Dietl killed for a while.

"Man, I could use another drink," he said.

"Wrong," Alda said. "There will be no more drinking while you're with me. Understand?"

"Have pity on me, woman," Nakai said, holding his head in his hands to slow the spinning and the pain. It didn't help much at all.

"Pity?" Alda said. "Maybe if you told me what was eating at you, I might have some pity."

Nakai shook his head and regretted it instantly. "I can't talk about it, and you wouldn't believe me if I did. No one does."

"Yeah," Alda said, the disgust clear in her voice. "Why would the woman who loves you ever believe you?" She snapped on the television as she headed for the door. "Just lay here and watch television while I get you some breakfast. Then we'll try that conversation again."

"Won't matter," Nakai said. "I still won't be able to . . ."

He let his voice trail off. Alda was already out of the room. He closed his eyes and lay back in the damp sheets. Instantly the bloody images rose in his mind.

"Bad choice," he muttered to himself, and opened his eyes. He had to focus on something. He made himself stare at the television. The road and desert scrub on the screen looked familiar. He felt himself snap to attention.

". . . appears these roads will not open anytime soon. The federal government is advising all county residents to stay indoors until further notice."

"What?" Alda said, coming back into the room and standing beside Nakai.

Nakai held up his hand for her to be silent.

The scene shifted to a reporter on location. Behind the reporter there was a roadblock, manned by army privates. Nakai didn't recognize any of the soldiers, but the road was one of the main roads leading into his base.

"Details are still sketchy," the reporter said. He was a slender well-dressed man who kept glancing over his shoulder nervously. Nakai had never seen a reporter who so clearly did not want to be on the scene. "Officials have confirmed that a large explosion destroyed Cole Army Base at 7:04 this morning. The size of this blast would seem to preclude the possibility of any survivors. At this moment the army is not saying what caused the explosion. It is currently under investigation."

"Oh, God," Alda said, covering her mouth as if she might throw up at any moment. She sank to the edge of the bed.

Nakai didn't move. He felt numb, not really believing that his entire base was gone, yet knowing exactly what the cause was.

There were no large-scale nukes on that base. And even if there were, they wouldn't have gone off randomly. There weren't any other weapons at the base that would be powerful enough to destroy it.

But Athelry had ordered the strange ship to be taken to one of the hangars at the base. There had probably been weapons in the thing.

Which meant that the explosion that destroyed the base might have been caused by the same thing that had killed Dietl.

Nakai's headache had just gotten worse.

Then his grandfather's words from the dream came back to him. He must stand up to the monster.

But he didn't want to. A monster like this was bigger than one man. Nakai couldn't handle something like this alone.

Alda moved closer to Nakai. She put her hand on his shoulder, trying to comfort him.

But what if his grandfather was right? What if it was Nakai's job to kill the monster? Why else would he have survived, not once, but twice? Why did he get away when Dietl hadn't? And why was he off the base when it was destroyed?

The monster would arrive spewing death from a shimmer in the air.

His grandfather had once said that to him.

You must stand against the blood. Allow your brother to stand with you.

The words from his dream. But what did they mean?

Alda slipped her arm around him. He leaned against her.

His father had been in that dream for a reason, laughing, holding bourbon. Nakai could be a laughing, drunken fool, or he could do something.

He had always vowed not to be like his father.

Nakai took a deep breath, and turned to Alda. "Can I borrow your car?"

"What for?" she asked, surprised.

"That was my base," he said, pointing at the television. "And I think I know what happened. It's my duty to go back."

"What if there's radiation?"

"They would be evacuating all areas downwind," Nakai said. "We would have heard by now. I'm going to go."

"There's nothing there, Enoch."

"You don't know that," he said. "*They* don't know that."

She gazed at him for a moment, as if she were trying to read his mind. "This is why you got drunk yesterday, isn't it?"

He nodded. "They sent me away. They shouldn't have."

"If they hadn't, you'd be dead now." Her voice shook, just a little.

"I know," he said. "I think I might have survived for a reason."

She leaned her forehead against his and sighed. Then she raised her head. "If you go, I'm coming with you."

"No," Nakai said. "There's no point in you exposing yourself to who knows what."

"But we're both safe right here," Alda said, the weight of her arm on his suddenly heavier, as if she might hold him down. "As far as the army knows, you're dead."

Nakai glanced at the television and then again remembered his grandfather's words. He had to stand up to the monster, fight what had destroyed his base, even if he died in the attempt.

"Even if you didn't go back," Alda said, "who would know?"

"*I* would know," Nakai said, feeling the rightness of the words. "And so would you."

12

The dream visit of our grandfather has helped my brother focus on the slaying of the monster. He thinks he is returning to the battle. What he does not know is that even if he had not returned, the battle would have come to him. The monster and the monster slayer both search for each other from the moment of their births. It is the way of things.

Sheriff Bogle had served as a New Mexico law officer for over twenty years, starting as a deputy right out of college and working his way up. He stood just over six feet, with broad shoulders and a disposition that made him laugh at troubles before he got angry at them. Everyone in the county knew him and liked him. And no one gave him any problems. They all knew that under his broad smile, weathered face, and twinkling eyes hid the sting of a scorpion.

But the scorpion wasn't hiding today. He'd already had a hell of a morning. After the army announced that the "earthquake" everyone had felt the day before had actually been an explosion that destroyed Cole Army Base in the next county, *his* county had gone crazy. Everyone who could was getting into cars, Jeeps, and rusted pickups, packing all they had, and was getting out of town. He'd never seen a traffic jam in Agate before, but he'd had to deal with one for most of the day.

He wasn't sure what they were afraid of—if there had been fallout from the explosion, the army would have issued warnings already and no one had. If there were going to be more explosions, they would be in the vicinity of the army base, not in Agate. But he couldn't explain that to anyone. No one wanted to hear logic.

Of course, he had to think logically because he had to stay. It was his job to serve and protect, and he was doing it. If he had children, though, or if his wife hadn't decided that rural New Mexico was too primitive for her, he would be shipping them out just as fast as he could. Hell, if the truth be told, he was jealous of the folks who had the ability to leave. He didn't. And neither did half the town.

Those who couldn't leave were watching the traffic jam with two parts envy and one part amusement. They stood in the doorways of their businesses, arms crossed, and made rude jokes, or catcalled the occasional fender bender. Not one of them went into the street to help—and that was damned unusual. In the past the locals had gone out of their way to help each other.

The only one who wasn't outside was Ben. He was sitting on the wrong side of his bar, sampling the wares. When Bogle had asked him if everything was all right, he had replied, "The army says so. Why should I doubt them?"

Why indeed? Bogle was asking himself just that question when the second oddity of the day occurred. The dispatch hailed him with news of a double murder at the Nadire place out on the old highway. Nadire was one of a dozen sheep herders who managed to stay alive in this area, spreading their flocks out over hundreds of acres of high desert to get them enough food. None of them or their kids had ever given him a whisper of trouble. There had never been petty theft or school-age pranks or even foul language from those families. He couldn't imagine how murder could occur up there.

Bogle had left two deputies in charge of making sure nothing got looted in town as everyone left, then picked up Dr. Ellison to head out to investigate. Ellison had been the county's only doctor for the last fifteen years. Everyone called him "Pro" instead of "Doc" because of his early days as a professional golfer. There wasn't a golf course within fifty miles of Agate, New Mexico, and Pro said he liked it just fine that way. From what the sheriff understood, Pro had given up golf after he broke just about all his clubs in a bad round during a Phoenix tournament. But in fifteen years he'd never heard Pro talk about that tournament or why he had moved to Agate.

Pro still half-looked like a golf professional. He always wore stylish short-sleeved shirts and slacks, and was very seldom seen without a golf hat on, even in the small county hospital. Despite his always looking so out of place, everyone in the county had grown to love him and his easy smile. Sheriff Bogle considered him more than a friend. The Pro was almost a partner in taking care of the county and all its residents.

The fifteen-minute ride out the old highway in the sheriff's Jeep was mostly silent. The warm morning air was swirling around the two men, both lost in their thoughts of losing Cole Army Base and facing a double-murder scene. Everything in their world had suddenly changed. It wasn't the sort of day for small talk.

The closer they got to the Nadire stake, the more Bogle dreaded it. He was beginning to wish he had never gotten up that morning. Finally, he saw the Nadire place on the side of the road. Nothing looked out of place. If he had been passing by, he wouldn't have noticed a thing.

Bogle slid the Jeep to a stop in the dirt of the Nadire driveway.

"Dan's truck?" Pro asked, pointing at the pickup parked in front of them.

"Yeah," Bogle replied. He didn't like the fact that Dan Bonner might be mixed up in this. Dan was one of the nicest people working for the big companies. He actually cared for these ranchers and herders in this area.

Walking Dove Nadire came slowly out the front door to greet them. She looked slumped over, as if simply standing was too much pain to endure. Normally she was a proud woman in her mid-forties who had raised her children to walk proud also. Now her weathered face was stained with tears and her eyes were empty.

"Back there," she said softly as Pro jumped out of the Jeep and moved to her. "Back there."

She was pointing to an area behind the house where the sheep were held.

"Can you tell me what happened?" Bogle asked. He didn't want to go barging around back there if the murderer might still be there waiting to gun them down.

"She's in shock," Pro said, steadying her with a firm hand.

Walking Dove shook her head from side to side, the tears flowing freely now. "I don't know," she said. "Billy saw everything."

"Billy?" Bogle asked.

"Their youngest son," Pro said. "About six. Sharp kid."

"Where's Billy?" Bogle asked.

"Inside," Walking Dove said softly.

At that moment a young child opened the screen door and stepped outside, letting the door bang closed behind him. The sound echoed over the surrounding desert and was carried away by the warm wind. Billy wore a Teenage Mutant Ninja Turtles T-shirt and stained jeans. He too had been crying, but at the moment he was trying to repress the tears.

His eyes weren't empty. Instead they had the thousand-yard stare that Bogle had seen countless times before, always on the faces of the vets who found refuge out here in the desert. Vets who had seen the worst of combat, whether in Korea, Vietnam, or the Gulf.

Bogle walked up the porch steps slowly, knowing if he moved too quickly the boy would bolt. Bogle waited until he had reached the boy's side before crouching so that he would be at the boy's eye level.

"Billy," Bogle said, making sure that he didn't patronize the kid. He was talking as one adult to another now, and he felt that would keep the kid calm. "Can you tell me what happened?"

Billy nodded, but kept his mouth closed.

Obviously this wasn't going to be easy. "What did you see?" Bogle asked, lowering his voice just a little, as if they were having an intimate conversation.

The boy blinked once, then said, "Blue fire."

"Blue fire?" Bogle repeated stupidly. He couldn't think what that meant.

Billy nodded again. "Just blue fire." His voice broke. He cleared his throat just like a man would do and said, "There was blue fire, and then Daddy was dead."

Bogle glanced up at Pro, who only shrugged.

"Did you see what caused the blue fire?" Bogle asked.

Billy shook his head.

"Blue fire," Bogle repeated, more to himself than to anyone else.

"And blood," the little boy said. The calm in his tone made Bogle shudder. "Lots of blood."

Bogle put a reassuring hand on the kid's shoulder, but he didn't know what to say. Even though he had been sheriff for a long time, he'd never spoken to a child who had just seen his father murdered. It would take a lot more time and effort to get a clearer picture from this boy.

Bogle took a deep breath. Whatever had caused that blue fire had to be long gone. It had taken him time to get here, and time must have elapsed before the dispatch took the call. But it was better to take precautions.

The sheriff squeezed Billy's shoulder. "You stay out here with your mother."

Billy nodded. Then Bogle stood, and unhooked the leather strap over his revolver. "Come on, Pro. Let's go take a look."

Pro gently patted Walking Dove's shoulder, then moved in behind Bogle as they headed past Dan's truck and toward the sheep pens.

It was instantly clear that something truly grisly had happened behind this herder's house. Blood was sprayed everywhere over the wooden sheep pen. It stained the dirt brown like raindrops. Human skin and intestines dripped from nearby sage. Even the remaining sheep in the pen had been splattered with blood and human skin.

What was left of Nadire's and Dan's bodies were just a few steps away from the pen. It was clear they had died almost instantly, literally blown apart by some intense force or weapon. That blue fire of Billy's was powerful stuff.

Bogle felt as if his stomach might give back the greasy breakfast he'd had a few hours before. In all his years he'd seen a lot of death, but nothing like this.

Bogle stopped a short distance from the bodies and held out his hand to stop Pro. "There's nothing you can do to help them," he said. "Let's not go messing up what evidence is there."

Pro only nodded, swallowing hard. It was clear to Bogle that even the doctor was sickened by this sight. Anyone would be.

"What kind of weapon could do this?" Pro asked.

"Not any weapon I'm familiar with," Bogle said. "I don't think it was a gun. I've never seen bullets do this kind of damage, not even a lot of them. If I didn't know better, I would say that it was an explosion. But there's no blast site."

"Well, if it wasn't a gun or a bomb," Pro said, "then what was it?"

A faint whirring filled the air, as if dozens of insects were swarming close by.

"You hear that?" Bogle asked.

"Yeah," Pro said. "Sounds like—"

Suddenly a red rope seemed to wrap around Pro's chest as if he'd been lassoed fifteen times. There was an intense crackle like electricity popping in a loose wire, and then Bogle heard the sizzle of flesh burning. The ropes were turning blue.

Blue energy.

Blue fire.

Pro let out a gagging cough as his eyes burst from their sockets, spraying blood over Bogle like someone had turned on two fire hoses. Pro was dead before his body hit the ground, his arms melted into the side of his body, smoke pouring from his mouth and nose.

The stink of burning flesh filled the air.

Bogle had his gun in his hands and was spinning around, looking for who or what had attacked his friend. His heart was pounding. Who'd've thought the killer would still be here? After all, the wife and kid were still alive. Didn't it know they were there? Or was it guarding the sheep pen?

He kept turning. There didn't seem to be anything, or anyone, around. Only the shimmering of the air between him and the house, like heat coming off the ground. But at that moment Bogle didn't feel much like waiting for a clear shot. It wasn't hot enough for the ground to be radiating heat waves, and in Bogle's mind, that meant that whatever had killed Pro had something to do with the shimmer.

He opened fire, spraying the area with shot after shot from his .357 Magnum.

And he hit nothing.

Or at least it seemed like nothing, until a hideous roar filled the air. Green liquid was spraying out in all directions. Bogle had hit something after all. Only he couldn't believe what he was seeing. A monster shimmered into view, holding its arm. A creature with long beaded hair and strange armor now faced him, holding one arm. It was big—bigger than anything he'd ever seen that stood on two legs.

Suddenly three red lights focused on Bogle's chest. He tried to move away, but before he could, a blue bolt of energy surged from a device beside the monster's ear. It hit Bogle instantly and sent him flying backward, his entire chest and stomach spraying out over the nearby brush and sheep, mixing with the blood of Nadire, Dan Bonney, and Dr. Ellison.

Bogle would never know exactly how much he had hurt the alien. But three of his shots had been lucky, destroying part of the alien's armor, and ripping through his skin and arm. It would slow the alien down for just long enough to save a few lives.

The alien moved over to Bogle's body, reached

down, and with a quick swipe of the wristblade severed the man's head from his body. Then, hanging
the sheriff's head on his belt, he turned and moved
off into the desert, green blood dripping from his
wounds.

13

My brother is Nayenezgani, the monster slayer. He is the chosen one, although he does not know it. He cannot know it, for to know it is to negate tradition. He must slay the monster for his own reasons, not because he is the chosen. And his reason is his family. Not his mother, his grandfather, or me. We have all gone to the next world. We visit him only in his dreams. We are his past. It is only for his future family that he must fight the monster.

Nakai pulled Alda's red-and-white Ford convertible over at the roadblock and shut off the engine. The heat of the day was now surrounding him, smothering him. The quiet of the desert filled the air almost as much as the heat, interrupted only by the sounds of a few engines and the police scanner echoing from one of the four cars forming the blockade.

Two state police officers were in the process of

helping a bus driver get his bus turned around on the narrow, two-lane highway. Nakai could see pale faces, like ghosts, staring out at the world behind the tinted bus windows. The bright sunshine and tinted windows made their faces look hollow, their eyes empty, as if the bus was full of the dead, just passing through the world of the living.

Nakai shook the image from his mind and headed for the state police sergeant standing near one of the cars. The sergeant was a burly man, with large arms and an even larger gut. Clearly he spent far more time behind the wheel of his cruiser than he spent walking or working out. He wore wrap-around sunglasses, but Nakai was sure that if he could see the sergeant's eyes, they would be small and black.

"Corporal Nakai, sir," he said without saluting. "I was stationed at Cole."

"Then you're a lucky one," the sergeant said without introducing himself or even pushing away from the patrol car he was leaning against. "Seems Cole no longer exists."

"I know," Nakai said. "That's why I need to get through. I can help the army's investigation into what happened."

"Sorry, son," the sergeant said. "No one gets past here."

"But you don't understand," Nakai said. "I'm stationed at Cole. I need to return."

"Like I said. Cole's not there anymore. So you got nothing to report back to now, do you?"

The cruelty in that statement made Nakai drawn in a sharp breath. He had lost friends at Cole. Didn't the man understand that?

And then the sergeant leaned forward and Nakai got an inkling of what the other man was trying to do.

"I understand one thing, Chief." The sergeant's last word was not a title. It was a slur. "I'm not in the army, and if I was, those hash marks make you a corporal, whereas I'm a sergeant."

Nakai started to interrupt the officer, but the big man held up his hand and pushed away from the patrol car with the other. "So you understand this," he said, moving up directly into Nakai's face. "As long as Uncle Sam says no one gets through, nobody gets through. So march your red butt back to your vehicle and move out. And that's an order!"

The last word he almost spit in Nakai's face. For an instant Nakai thought of taking the fat man to his knees, but this didn't seem to be the fight he should be picking at the moment. Without a word he spun and walked away.

Fat racist pig. The sergeant didn't have a shred of human dignity and he was making sure Nakai knew it. Alda had been right. He didn't owe the army anything. In a day or so he'd make a few calls to let them know he was alive. And if they wanted to talk to him, he would talk. But chances were that it wouldn't make any difference. By then they would either know what had blown up the base, or they would think they knew.

He spun the car around and headed back down the road. At the intersection with Highway 36 he pulled into the dusty parking lot of Rosalita's Diner. Rosalita's slogan was "Rib-Stickin' Food for Hard-working People," and she did offer some of the best meals in the area. The diner itself was nothing to look at—a squat, dusty building in the middle of the scrub. People who were used to city food wouldn't even stop, but as a result they missed one of the better truck stops in New Mexico.

Usually a dozen or so trucks filled the huge gravel parking lot behind the diner. Today, there were only two cars in front. It must have been too close to Cole for most people's comfort. Besides, the truckers were probably worked up about the police barricades. And the way the media was reporting things, the entire area sounded like it was going to disappear at a moment's notice.

Nakai pulled himself out of the convertible without opening the door. He crossed the gravel lot and climbed the steps, thankful that Rosalita's pay phone was outside. He didn't want to face her today.

The pay phone's receiver was hot to the touch. Nakai held it in two fingers as he punched Alda's number with his other hand. Twenty seconds later Alda answered the phone, and her pleasure and relief at hearing his voice made him smile.

It took him just a minute to tell her about the scene on the highway with the police. "So I don't have a choice, really," he finished saying. "I'll be back in a half an hour or so."

"The sooner the better," Alda said. "This entire town is spooked."

"I am too," Nakai told her. "A situation like this would spook anyone."

"There's more," Alda said, and Nakai glanced around at the empty parking lot as the dread filled his stomach. How could there be more?

"Sheriff Bogle and Dr. Ellison were killed this morning out by the old highway. A sheep herder's wife drove into town with the news, telling everyone to lock their doors. She was taking her children and getting out of Agate for good.''

''Killed?'' Nakai said, more to himself than to Alda. Then he added. ''Do you know how?''

''I was at work when she came into town,'' Alda said. ''She didn't say how they were killed, just that they were lucky to get out, but her son kept repeating 'blue fire, blue fire,' over and over.''

Even with the heat of the parking lot, Nakai shuddered. The thing that had killed Dietl was still alive, and moving. The blue fire was still killing.

''Honey,'' he said, his voice as cold and harsh as he could make it. ''Listen to me. Get the hell out of that town. Now!''

''What are you talking about?'' Alda said. ''I can't go anywhere. You've got the car.''

Nakai glanced around at the convertible behind him, then quickly came up with a plan. ''Just catch a ride with someone down Highway 36 until you get to Rosalita's. The car will be here. You still have the spare set of keys, don't you?''

''Yeah,'' Alda said, ''but I—''

He didn't let her finish. ''Now, just listen to me. Take the car across the border into Arizona as fast as you can and don't stop for anything. You've been wanting to visit your sister in Phoenix. Go there and I'll call you when things are safe here.''

''But why?'' Alda asked.

For a moment Nakai thought he couldn't tell her. Then he realized that everyone who had sworn him to secrecy was dead. ''Because that same blue fire was near the army base, and it killed people there, too.''

"And then the base exploded," Alda whispered.

"That's right," Nakai said.

"But all the people here—"

"Will be fine if I do what I plan."

"Then I can stay."

"*No!*" The two diners in Rosalita's looked through the window at the sound of Nakai's voice. He turned his back and faced the parking lot. "I can't do what I have to do if I'm worried about you. Please, trust me on this. I love you. Do this for me."

There was a moment of silence on the phone, then Alda asked, "Where will you be?"

Nakai glanced at the open desert across the highway, back in the direction of the roadblock and the base. "I'm going to head down to what's left of Cole."

"But why?" Alda said. "Why not come to Phoenix with me?"

"There will be an army team there to investigate the explosion. I know more about the situation than they do. They need me. With my help, the army can stop whatever is doing the killing."

Again there was a moment of silence on the phone. Finally Alda said softly, "Be careful."

"I will," Nakai said. "But I want you out of the area first. Okay? Promise me I'll find you at your sister's in Phoenix."

He held his breath for a moment. Alda took promises very seriously. If she promised, she would do what he asked.

"I promise," Alda said.

"Good," Nakai said. "Now get going. I'll call you as soon as I can."

With that he hung up the phone and glanced

around the hot, dusty parking lot. Cars were already starting to stream past, families fleeing Agate and the death that hung over this area.

He turned and headed into Rosalita's. He needed a meal and a lot of water, and then he would be ready.

The dinners looked at him warily as he came in, but Rosalita greeted him as if he were an old friend. He ordered a blue-plate special and four bottles of water. Rosalita looked at him as if he were crazy, but he explained that they were for later. She brought them to his place at the counter, ice-cold plastic bottles with a bit of condensation on the sides, and he knew he had to ration them. They would be all he had to get him through the desert.

He ate the blue-plate special so fast he barely tasted it. When he was done, he placed enough cash to cover the meal and the tip on top of the order ticket, grabbed his water, and left.

He walked past Alda's car, hoping it wouldn't be there when he returned. If he came back this way. Then he crossed the highway and headed out into the desert, angling away from the road. He would give the police roadblocks plenty of room.

He moved through the brush and cactus just as he had done his entire life. Out there, under the hot sun of the high desert, he felt more at home than in any other place on earth. This was his land and he knew it. Somewhere out on this desert was a monster that killed his friends. He would find the monster and kill it.

Or he would die trying.

14

In any hunt, the hunter and the prey are drawn together by forces beyond their understanding. It is the way of the world. Often, the time is not yet right for the hunter to hunt. Or for the prey to die. That too is the way of things.

The sun had set over an hour before, but the heat of the day still filled the desert air. For Nakai, the afternoon had been a long one. He had managed no more than eight miles through the rough terrain, swinging at least three miles wide of the roadblock that had stopped him earlier in the day. The water had helped. He rationed it. He still had two full bottles tucked in the waistband of his pants. He had kept the other two empty bottles as well; the admonition he had learned as a boy not to leave anything in the desert was ingrained too deep to change.

He'd had long stretches where he could think

about things like that—the lessons he had learned growing up in the high desert—but those long stretches were punctuated by moments of terror. Planes and helicopters flew overhead in an obvious search pattern. Several times he had been forced into hiding under brush and in rock piles. One helicopter had passed within fifty feet, the wash from the props kicking up dirt and dust, covering him where he hid under a rock outcropping. The federal government wanted all access to Cole Army Base closed off, that was for sure. And not only were they blocking the roads, but they were flying close patrols of the perimeter of the base.

Normally, the patrols would have spotted anyone trying to do what he was doing. But he was Navajo, born and raised in this high desert. The open space wasn't open to the eyes of someone who knew what he was looking at. And Nakai knew it all. He could blend into a brush pile or melt into the rocks faster than any plane could catch him. And he moved through the brush without a sound, his steps silent on the sand and dirt.

Ahead a few miles he could see the lights of the temporary army base set up outside of where Cole had been. That proved that the explosion hadn't been nuclear. They would never have set up this close if it had been. The army might have risked the enlisted men forty years ago, but not now.

It was no more than ten o'clock in the evening and the white-and-orange lights filled the night sky, pushing back the stars. Nakai figured he would be in the base within the hour, taking his time to make sure he didn't get stopped by any sentries.

He stopped to take a sip from one of his precious

warm bottles. The bottled water was his only conces-
sion to modern times. His grandfather would have
laughed at Nakai's need for water. His grandfather
would have argued that Nakai should have prepared
for such an emergency long before. But Nakai
hadn't. And he had been drunk the night before;
and alcohol dehydrates the body. His need for water,
if anything, was much greater than it had been.

The water was hot, but tasted good. He made
sure that his sip was a small one. He still wasn't certain of his reception at the base.

Strange that they put the new camp so close to
the old one. The lights almost made it look as if the
old camp remained.

It was as he was looking at the lights ahead that
out of the corner of his eye he caught a slight yellow
flicker of another light, this one much, much closer.

Crouching and moving silently through the
night, he headed toward the flicker, moving silently
up the slope. About halfway up the slope he caught
the familiar odor of a campfire. Yet mixed with the
fire was no smell of cooking food. And on such a
warm evening, the camper didn't need a fire for
heat. Very curious.

Nakai moved slowly, making sure to keep the
hill between himself and the fire, making sure he
remained downwind, never making a noise. It took
him almost twenty minutes before he managed to
crawl silently over the slight rise into a position
where he could see the fire.

It took him a moment to realize what he was
seeing. The blaze itself was small, contained between
a few rocks. Sheriff Bogle's head—hat, sunglasses,
and all—sat on a rock, staring at the fire. Next to

Bogle was the head of Dr. Ellison. His eyes and jaw were gone, but his usual golf hat remained firmly in place. Three other heads were beside the two, including Private Dietl's.

Nakai wanted to gag, but didn't.

Sitting on the far side of the fire was a monster like none that he had ever seen or imagined in his worst, drunken nightmares. The monster was covered in armor and thick, hidelike skin, with what looked like a helmet sitting on the rock beside him. The monster had an antlike face, with large mandibles that angled inward. At the corners of his mouth were large fangs. This mouth was powerful, and terrifying. It was made all the worse by the creature's nearly human eyes. Thick strands of ropelike hair flowed around his head, seemingly decorated with strangely fashioned beads.

Nakai held his breath. This was the source of the blue fire. Something that preyed on man. Nakai squinted, and frowned as he did so. This creature had the ability to camouflage itself, to so blend in with its surroundings that not even Nakai could see it. But it wasn't trying to hide itself now.

Nakai's mouth was dry despite the water he had just sipped. He wondered if this was how a deer felt when it stumbled on a hunter's camp. The thought made him shudder. Those heads—the remains of people he had known—were placed around that campfire like trophies.

With clawed fingers, the monster seemed to be working on an instrument panel strapped to his arm. Even in the faint light Nakai could gather that the monster's arm had been wounded and the panel damaged.

Nakai took all this in with a glance and his first impulse was to run, as fast and as far as he could. But he knew from experience that this monster was fast. If he ran, the monster would see and hear him and more than likely cut him down before he reached a safe distance.

Using his grandfather's training, Nakai took a slow, shallow breath, his muscles taut and ready to move instantly. He had managed to get this close without being seen; he could manage to move away. It would be his only hope.

Slowly, Enoch, slowly, he thought, over and over. He made the thought into a mantra, something that would keep him focused.

Slowly, Enoch, slowly.

With another shallow breath, Nakai backed away from the edge of the hill, never taking his gaze off the monster in front of him. He moved an inch at a time, not worrying about his speed, only about his safety.

Shallow breath, then another inch back.

The monster continued to work on the instrument panel on his arm.

Slowly, Enoch, slowly.

The monster pressed a talon against the armband.

Nakai moved another inch, took another breath.

The monster shook his arm slightly.

Nakai was just about to drop back out of the monster's range of vision when disaster struck. A small rock near his right boot dislodged and bounced down the slope, kicking a slightly larger rock loose.

To Nakai, it sounded as if cannons had been fired in the quiet desert air.

Instantly the monster looked up, saliva dripping from its jaws, its eyes staring into the darkness. It was looking in Nakai's direction, but Nakai wasn't sure if he had been seen.

He certainly had been heard.

Nakai moved silently down out of the monster's sight path, then over and behind a large rock. His only hope was that the monster couldn't see through solid stone.

Nakai pressed himself into position against the boulder, ready to spring out at the instant the monster found him. He knew his only hope if discovered was to attack.

The monster kicked a rock loose as he climbed from his fire toward the top of the hill. But it was only a small pebble. The monster knew how to move as silently as Nakai.

To Nakai's right there was another noise. Faint, like a man walking barefoot over a soft carpet.

Nakai's senses were taking in everything. He could smell the rotting odor of the monster and another odor, faint, but definitely there. There had been another creature on the ridge with Nakai. Sitting as quiet as Nakai had tried to be. And now that the monster was moving, the other creature was moving.

The warm wind swirled, bringing the distinctive odor of cat to Nakai.

Puma. Big devil cat.

Nakai held himself frozen against the rock, not daring to move a muscle. He'd seen his share of the big cats over the years and had no desire to tangle with one.

As the three warriors stalked one another, the night sky seemed to swell with the intense silence of the desert night, the only background sound the slight wind in the dry brush.

The monster cleared the top of the ridge, stopping just quickly enough that Nakai could hear the sound of the heavy steps in the sand. Unless the creature could see through rock, Nakai was hidden for the moment. But with another few steps, it would see him even in the faint light.

Suddenly a low growl filled the night air. A growl so close above Nakai's head that it sent shivers down his spine, almost forcing him to jump and run. Somehow he managed to remain still. He had learned many times from his grandfather that a warrior's best and most valuable skill was the ability to remain unseen. At the moment his only chance of survival was being invisible.

The growl shook the desert as it grew into an angry roar, seeming to echo off the stars themselves.

The monster shifted quickly as the big cat jumped from its hiding place. Nakai could hear the struggle as the cat's razor-sharp claws scraped against armor. Then there was a loud crunch as the cat bit into the monster, who let out an unearthly scream of anger.

Nakai glanced around the edge of the rock. The creature sprang away from the big cat, leaping a good ten feet away with seeming ease.

But the big cat, smelling the rot and the blood of its enemy wasn't going to be stopped. It had singled out its prey and it would die taking it down if it had to. With the monster firing, the big cat again attacked, this time going for the throat.

The monster fired back, blue bolts of energy grazing the cat in mid-leap, but not stopping it. The cat's weight was too much for the monster and the two combatants rolled in the rocks, the red blood of the cat mixing with the dark blood of the alien.

Nakai knew the outcome, knew the cat wouldn't win. But the cat had saved his life. If Nakai moved now. *Only* if he moved now.

Turning from the battle, he headed down the hill at full run, not allowing himself even to glance backward. He put both hands on his water bottles, holding them in place. He didn't want to lose them, not here, not now. If that thing came farther into the desert, the last thing Nakai wanted was to give it a trail to follow.

With that in mind, he leaped over some small rocks, made sure he varied his steps so that his footprints didn't lead directly anywhere.

And while he did that, he ran. And as he did, he silently thanked his grandfather for all the training. All the training Nakai had rebelled against as a young boy.

Two more bolts of blue light lit up the desert, and this time it was the cat who screamed in agony.

As rapidly and as silently as he could run, Nakai headed for the distant light of the army encampment. Behind him another blue flame lit up the night, then the silence closed back in over the desert as if nothing had happened.

The battle was over. The devil cat had lost. But clearly it had taken its toll on the monster.

Never missing a step, making as little noise as

possible, Nakai ran on. He now knew what his enemy looked like. And, more important, he knew his enemy could bleed.

If his enemy could be wounded, he could be killed. And Nakai wanted to be the one to do it.

15

A true hunter must know what weapons to use for each creature. A hunter does not go after a small bird with a tree stump. Or attack a running buffalo with only his fists. But even with the correct weapon, the ultimate outcome always turns on the ability of the hunter to outthink his prey.

Nakai's heart had stopped racing and he had caught his breath long before he reached the outside perimeter of the army encampment. Before he went in, he finished off the third bottle of water, figuring after his near miss in the desert, he needed it.

The army had decided to set up their headquarters in a small valley, just above where Cole Army Base used to be. Even in the moonlight, he could see the changes: the desert glittered like a billion stars, the sand fused by the intense heat of the explosion into a field of glass globules reflecting the moon.

Nakai would have thought they'd have set up the camp farther away, but apparently those in charge knew more than he did.

He climbed silently up toward a shallow saddle among some large rocks. Two guards sat near a fire. The smell of coffee filled the night, making Nakai's stomach rumble slightly. Except for the blue-plate special at Rosalita's, he hadn't had anything at all to eat for almost twelve hours. He was going to need some more food soon to replenish his strength.

Nakai moved up to a point twenty feet from the two guards. The firelight brought both their faces into clear perspective, just as the monster's fire had illuminated him. Nakai found it strange that this fire calmed him, while the other had terrified him, even before he had seen the creature warming itself before its flames.

Nakai crouched and stared, taking in the entire scene. These two guards were the only men on this part of the perimeter.

One of the men wore black-rimmed glasses, while the other had deep-set eyes and a heavy mustache. It seemed that the one with glasses was supposed to be walking post, but had stopped for the moment. A moment was just enough time for Nakai to get through easily.

"Say, Figueras," the one with glasses said, kneeling by the fire. "How about another cup of java? I got more than an hour to go and I can hardly keep my eyes open."

"You're still on watch, Private," the one sitting by the fire said, his voice deep and strong. "The major will kill you if he sees you off post."

"Man, I can hardly stay awake enough to walk,"

the man in glasses said just as Nakai moved past them, silently creeping through the dark night toward the camp below. "Besides, that's a bomb crater over there. People died there, and they don't know exactly what kind of weapon caused it. Ain't no one in his right mind who'd want to be within miles of this spot."

Nakai completely agreed with the private. No sane person would want to be here. But at the moment he knew he was far from sane. There was a monster out there in that desert and that monster had to be dealt with. His run-in with it only increased his respect for it—and his determination to wipe it off the planet.

Gradually the guards' voices faded. Nakai moved along the edge of the blast crater, keeping down. It was harder to walk here, harder to keep silent. The terrain was forever altered by that explosion. He didn't even want to think about the toxins or other bomb residue he was exposing himself to. He would worry about that later. Right now he would comfort himself with the thought that the army wouldn't place tents so close to a dangerous site.

Yeah. Right.

It took him about ten minutes to reach the camp. No one saw him. No one tried to stop him. For that, he was relieved, and a bit worried. If they didn't see him, a man who couldn't make himself invisible, they would never be able to see the monster. That creature had better stealth capabilities than anything the Department of Defense designed.

As Nakai made his way through the tents, he noted their configuration. Anyone who understood the army would know automatically where the colonel's tent would be. Anyone who understood the army knew, of course, that a colonel would be the man with the highest rank here. Anytime there was danger, the army would send in a colonel to secure the place before risking the generals.

The colonel's tent was right where Nakai thought it would be. The tent was larger than all the others, of course. It had three sentries on post around it, and inside, a meeting was going on, the light casting odd shadows on the tent. Nakai moved past one sentry without making a sound. The sentry was so oblivious he didn't even notice Nakai's movement in the dark. The army should have its guards trained by men like his grandfather, not the rigid officers who ran the boot camps. The officers created grunts. Nakai's grandfather had taught survival.

Nakai cut along the edge of the tent. From inside, he could hear voices, some clearer than others. One voice broke over the rest. "I understand what you're saying, sir. The Geiger counters all show very low radiation readings at ground zero, but I'm still hesitant to send men in."

Nakai nodded to himself. That explained why the camp was so close. The monster's explosion had carried very little radiation with it. He felt more relief than he wanted to acknowledge.

The voice went on. "I believe our aerial photographs make it clear that a powerful weapon of some sort was used on the base. A closer inspection is unlikely to yield more data at this time."

"I disagree, Major," another voice said as Nakai neared the front flap of the tent. This voice was deeper and clearly carried more authority. "We're still operating in the dark here, and any bit of information we can glean from the blast site is of the utmost importance."

Nakai took a deep breath. It was time for him to tell his story. He hoped they would listen to him before they arrested him.

He stepped toward the light coming from the tent and went under the open flap. He put his hands up and in clear view for good measure.

"Begging the colonel's pardon, sir," Nakai said as he walked all the way inside.

There were five men in the large tent and four of them instantly drew pistols, aiming them at him. Only the bald-headed colonel sitting at a paper-covered table didn't move.

Nakai stopped, waiting. The interior of the tent smelled of sweat, fear, and cigarette smoke.

"How'd you get in here?" a major with red hair barked, his gun not wavering.

"I walked into camp, sir," Nakai said. "And the door to the tent was open."

"All right, son," the colonel said. "Slowly step into the light and identify yourself." Then, glancing around at the four guns leveled at Nakai, he added, "And if I were you, I'd make sure my hands remained visible."

Nakai stepped forward and snapped to attention. "Corporal Enoch Nakai, sir. Permanently stationed at Cole—until yesterday, that is."

The colonel rose and moved around the table toward Nakai, motioning for the others to put away their weapons. "You mean to tell me you managed to escape that blast?"

"I had a three-day pass, sir," Nakai said.

"Then why in God's name did you come back here?" The colonel was only inches from him.

"Because, sir, they sent me away. They felt I knew too much."

"Knew too much?" The colonel's eyes narrowed. "You *knew* that this blast was going to happen?"

One of the men brought his gun back up.

"No, sir," Nakai said, keeping his eye on the gun. "But I know what caused it."

"You do?"

"Yes, sir," Nakai said. "I was there when they brought the craft in, and I've seen the pilot."

"Craft? Pilot?" the colonel said. He turned to the major. "Has anyone thought to look through the last few days of reports sent to headquarters from Cole?"

The major looked perplexed, then motioned to a corporal, who hurriedly left the tent.

"We'd been operating under the assumption that some of Cole's own equipment malfunctioned," the colonel said. "At least, we were hoping that happened. Are you saying this was a terrorist act?"

"It's not that simple, sir," Nakai said.

The colonel nodded, as if pieces he hadn't understood were beginning to come together. He pushed the officer's gun down and pulled out a chair. "Son, it looks as if you have a story to tell us about this explosion."

"I do, sir," Nakai said. "But believe me, sir, the blast that destroyed the base is the least of our problems."

16

My twin bother is Nayenez-gani, *the monster slayer. He learned his art at our grandfather's knee. Our grandfather taught him many things: how to track through the desert; how to remain hidden; and how to lure a monster. This last is important. Before the monster can be slain, it must be found. Sometimes a good hunter must use bait to lure the monster into the light. A good hunter never worries about the well-being of his bait.*

The sun broke over the bubbled, glasslike plain that had been Cole Army Base. The cool morning air felt refreshing, but Nakai knew the coolness wouldn't last long. He ran a hand through his buzz-cut hair and stretched. He was doing remarkably well for a man who had traveled across a desert in the heat of the day. It felt good to unburden himself, finally, to people who believed him.

Last night it had taken him over two hours to explain everything that had happened, from Dietl's death to the fight between the monster and the big cat. In the middle of his story, the major returned with faxed documents in his hands. They were copies of the reports filed in Washington during the last night of Cole Army Base. It was strange to see Sergeant Coates's name and Colonel Athelry's signature. Neither man would bother him anymore. Strangely, Nakai was not glad for that. He wouldn't miss them, but he was sorry that they had died. He only hoped their deaths had been quick.

The faxes had arrived at the critical point in Nakai's retelling. The colonel had stopped, read the documents, and said only, "It seems that you weren't the only one who found this craft unusual. Washington sent in some of our top brains to decipher what in the hell it was."

"Had they arrived?" Nakai asked, afraid he knew the answer.

The colonel nodded, then set the faxes down. He had gazed out the open door at the crater. So many lives, gone in an instant. After a moment's reflection, the colonel had signaled Nakai to continue.

He had complied, talking for another hour. Then he ended his story by telling the colonel that he could track the pilot of the alien craft through the desert. He would need a vehicle, weapons, and a few extra men and nothing more. Much to Nakai's surprise, the colonel had agreed to the plan, ordering Major Lee to lead it and help Nakai.

Nakai glanced around the encampment, then headed for the staging area, where the humvees waited for him. How different it was to have a colonel who believed him implicitly, who listened to everything he said. Nakai only wished that it had come about some other way.

Six short hours after Nakai had told his story, everything was ready. Even that surprised him. He had expected it to take more time. But the colonel had understood everything, especially the urgency.

There had been a late-night planning session, and then Nakai was given his own tent to bunk in. He hadn't managed to get any sleep, but he had rested. He knew he wouldn't sleep until the monster was dead. Or he was.

Nakai stepped up to the back of one humvee and picked out an M-16, slinging it over his shoulder. The only other thing he grabbed was a full canteen. Those bottles of water had saved him, but they had certainly been awkward.

"Ready, Corporal?" Major Lee asked as he walked up to the humvee. His face was red from the desert sun, as if he had already spent too much time outside. Nakai didn't want to tell him that he might be wise to get some suntan lotion on that pale skin. But it was Lee's pale skin. He should have known the damage the desert sun wrought on white men.

"Ready, sir," Nakai said.

"Then let's do it."

Nakai nodded. He knew the other men thought this part of the plan strange, but Nakai had insisted. He had to go on foot. Traveling any other way would obscure what tracks he had made the night before. The humvees would follow, for backup and for a hasty getaway.

Without another word, Nakai turned and started up the slope. His muscles were stiff from his walk the day before, but he figured it wouldn't take much to loosen them. As he headed across the desert, he reflected on how much easier it was to travel when he didn't have to worry about being silent. He back-tracked his path from the night before, realizing that he needn't have worried about not finding it. The memory of his trek was so clear to him that he recognized every bit of scrub.

The two vehicles carrying Major Lee and six men followed a close distance behind, ready to move up into position at any moment and give Nakai cover. Nakai didn't expect to need any help for some time. He doubted the monster was still in the same place, but that was where Nakai had last seen him, and that was where Nakai had to start his chase.

It took less than an hour to find the creature's camp, now abandoned and cold. The puma's body lay broken and skinned on the rocks. Flies and ants ate at the exposed muscle and flesh. One of the human heads had been left behind on a rock, almost as if taunting Nakai. It was Sheriff Bogle's, sunglasses and wide-brimmed hat still in place.

This creature was smart. It had left the most identifiable head, just to make a point.

When the major saw the severed head he turned even whiter, but didn't lose his breakfast, as two of the men with him did.

Nakai glanced at the two men, then turned to the major. "If this makes them sick, you may want to leave them behind. What lies ahead will be much, much worse."

Major Lee nodded in agreement, then ordered his men to scout the surrounding area while he called in a helicopter with more men to secure the site. It took twenty minutes for reinforcements to arrive.

While he waited, Nakai scouted the surrounding area. The monster was smart. It had left a number of false trails. But it hadn't known how to fool an expert tracker, at least not in this landscape. Nakai found the real trail fast enough, and even though he had expected it, he still felt a shiver run down his back.

The creature had gone back to Agate.

Nakai hoped to hell that Alda had taken his advice and gotten out. He hoped she had taken her friends with her.

When Nakai came back, he must have looked a bit stunned, because the major frowned at him.

"Problems?"

Nakai wasn't going to answer that. Instead, he said, "I found the trail."

"Good," Lee said, and turned away. He finished securing the area, then traded the two men who had lost their breakfast for a couple of sturdier stomachs. When the men were in place, Lee gave the go-ahead.

Nakai didn't even hesitate.

He went south, walking quickly toward the small town of Agate twenty miles away. Behind him the humvees followed, as if he were leading his own parade. A very deadly parade.

The monster's tracks didn't change direction for almost fifteen miles. It had made the trek last night, after the fight, under cover of darkness. But as it approached Agate, the monster had veered from cover to cover, clearly working its way into the town. Nakai hoped that everyone in Agate was gone to safer areas. If not, there more than likely were more bodies and heads waiting to be found.

It took the group most of the day to cover this stretch of desert. That was fine as far as Nakai was concerned. Attacking the creature at night might give them a bit of an advantage. It had a way of becoming invisible to the eye in daylight.

When they reached the highway, Nakai made the group stop. He waited a long time, to see if there was any traffic. There wasn't. He wasn't sure if that was a good or a bad sign. Then, at his signal, they crossed the highway and stopped at Henry Barber's gas station. They moved the humvees around back and into the shade. Henry had locked the doors and put up a "Closed" sign on the door. Nothing had disturbed the place.

Nakai figured that the monster was doing the same as they were doing: holing up in a safe spot and resting during the last few hot hours of the day, then hunting at night. It was apparent to Nakai after witnessing last night's fight with the cat that the monster had the ability to see in the darkness. Some sort of night vision or infrared ability. But it was also clear that the monster could be killed. And that was exactly what Nakai intended to do.

The time passed slowly, but finally the sun dropped below the horizon and Agate's few street-lights came on. Nakai forced himself to wait at least another half hour, then motioned to Major Lee that they should be starting out.

Just as they were ready, a red sports car sped past, heading into town. It was the first car they'd seen in the past two hours. From what Nakai could tell in the waning light, there was a driver behind the wheel and another man slouched in the passenger seat.

"Our bait," Nakai said to the major, hoping that the bait would serve more as a lure than as the strange predator's first kill of the evening.

The major nodded, but looked a bit uncomfortable. Nakai was beyond that now. He had to get this monster before it got them. He swung up into the back of the humvee and grabbed a rocket launcher. "Follow with lights off. Keep our distance."

The major gave the order and they pulled out, making sure the sports car's taillights were a good distance ahead in the small town of Agate.

17

In any war, warriors die. Innocents die. My brother is in a war with the monster. There have been many deaths. There will be many more. It is the nature of war.

The cool breeze from the air-conditioning filled the red sports car, keeping Jay Newport and Scott Richards comfortable in the hot desert evening. Jay's stereo played one of his favorite tapes, *The Best of the Bee Gees*, loud enough to drown out the sounds of the motor. Scott hated the tape and the group, but over the long trip from Phoenix, they had agreed to alternate music. At the moment it happened to be Jay's turn and Scott was doing his best to ignore the awful sounds.

Jay had the classic looks of a television anchorman. His thick brown hair, even in a wind, always seemed to be in perfect order, and his brown eyes were full, almost doelike. Cameras loved him, but television station executives hadn't liked his attitude so far. He wanted to be in charge and usually acted as if he knew everything. It was the worst attitude a young anchor could have, forcing Jay to remain in the lower levels of the industry, looking for that big break that would jump him up. So far, he hadn't found it.

Scott was the opposite of Jay. He worked simply for the money, running cameras and equipment because it was easy for him to do. His true love was his art, a complex mix of pottery and sculpture that hadn't sold, as of yet. But every spare minute he kept at it, knowing his work would someday be discovered. In the meantime he worked at the station and did his best to avoid trips like this one with Jay.

This trip would make him avoid any that required a lot of driving. Next time he would insist on flying. *The Best of the Bee Gees* was bad enough, but when it was combined with *Frampton Comes Alive* and *Barry Manilow's Greatest Hits,* it made the experience into a seventies flashback that was driving Scott crazy. He was trying to counter it with Smashing Pumpkins, Nirvana, and Hole, but somehow that didn't annoy Jay. Although he would find reasons to stop more often when Scott's music was on.

Scott could use a stop now. It had been over two hours and the warm Diet Coke he had bought south of here was long gone. All he wanted was a meal and a place to sleep—even though he knew he suspected the Brothers Gibb, and not Courtney Love, would be providing the soundtrack for tonight's dreams.

Jay had picked Agate off a New Mexico map as

the place to stop. It was one of the few towns near Cole Army Base. Scott sincerely hoped that Agate wasn't one of those one-horse towns so common in the high desert. He really didn't want to backtrack.

They were going to try to get inside army lines around Cole Army Base. Jay needed footage, and he brought Scott, who'd actually had some journalism experience under combat conditions in the Gulf. That was before he decided to concentrate on his art. He wished Jay didn't know about it, though. Jay figured that if Scott had gotten behind military lines in the Gulf, where the restrictions were tough, he'd be able to do the same in the States. The problem was that Jay wanted Scott to take him along for the ride.

Scott suspected that they wouldn't get in, but he didn't know how to tell Jay. He was waiting until they pulled into Agate before he broached the topic.

Although, he had to admit, the next day wasn't his highest priority at the moment. It had been bothering him that they hadn't seen any traffic for hours now. Jay had explained it away simply: Would you want to drive to the site of a recent explosion? But Scott didn't buy it. After all, tons of folks drove to see the mess after the Oklahoma City bombing, and that was before they knew what caused it. They should have been passing a small contingent of sickos, wackos, and the unrelentingly curious. And then, added to that, the dramatic outpouring of cars they had seen that morning—cars with everything from chairs to bed frames tied to their hoods—made it all seem more dangerous than they had anticipated.

Scott didn't like this. And, as they reached the

edge of Agate, and didn't see anyone moving in the streets, he liked it even less.

"Man, this place looks like it's been abandoned," Scott said, turning down the music as Jay slowed to Agate's posted thirty-five-mile-per-hour speed limit.

"It's only a little past nine," Jay said. "Even these local yokels don't roll up the sidewalks this early."

The sidewalks, hell. The sidewalks had debris on them: dolls, bits of clothing, loose papers. The streets were completely empty.

"No cars," Scott said, his voice suddenly very soft. "There aren't any cars anywhere."

"Shit," Jay said, looking both left and right, staring into the night. "You're right."

The door of a place called Ben's Saloon was swinging back and forth in the slight wind. It was an eerie look, like someone was still there, trying to get in and out.

"This town has been abandoned," Scott said. "Why?"

"And there's our story," Jay said, pounding on the steering wheel with his fist and laughing. "We fell right into it."

"Yeah," Scott said. "That's one perspective." He could think of a hundred others. Like the fact that he should have been paying more attention to his feelings on that empty highway.

"You know," Scott said, "there are times you've got to trust your gut."

"My gut says that this is a story we can sell to the network," Jay said.

"Maybe," Scott said. "But the entire town's

abandoned. Don't you think the network would have been here for a story like that? CNN would have."

"If they knew," Jay said.

"Yeah. That's another perspective."

"You keep saying that," Jay snapped. "Why?"

"Because," Scott said, "even the network would keep its reporters away from a place giving off high levels of radiation."

"Nah," Jay said, brushing aside Scott's comment with a wave of his hand, like brushing away a fly. He slowed the car down to a crawl to stare at the abandoned storefronts. "I checked the winds over Cole and they're all heading the other direction. Even if there was radiation, it wouldn't be coming here."

"So why is everyone gone?" Scott asked.

"When we know that," Jay said, "we have our story."

Suddenly, out of the corner of his eye, Scott caught movement. He slowed the car to almost a crawl between the two-story buildings that lined the main street of Agate. "Did you see something?"

Jay stared in the direction Scott was looking, then shook his head. "Nothing." Then Jay laughed. "You must be seeing ghosts or—"

A huge creature jumped from out of the shadows, landing right in front of the red sports car.

"Holy jumping shit!" Jay shouted.

"Get us out of here!" Scott yelled.

Jay slammed his foot on the gas, sending the car fishtailing ahead, around the monster, who just stood there, staring at them through a helmetlike face mask. Scott got a sense of broad strength and power and incredible size before he turned his head back to see why the damn car was fishtailing. The back end of the car spun wide, then Jay recovered and the car shot ahead.

"What was that?" Scott shouted He glanced around, but the creature was nowhere to be seen.

Suddenly the creature jumped in front of the car again. The thing was huge. And it had talons.

"How in the hell did it do that?" Jay shouted as he swerved the car to the right, jumping up on the curb to miss the creature. The rear of the car clipped a garbage can and Jay fought to keep it accelerating ahead.

Scott was bracing himself against the dash. In all his years he hadn't been this scared. He wished he were driving. He could at least get them out of there.

"Don't hit that thing!" he yelled.

"I won't," Jay screamed back.

"And don't stop!" Scott squinted. The creature was gone.

"Why the hell would I stop?" Jay yelled.

Again the creature landed in front of the car.

"Shit!" Jay shouted, yanking the car to the right, just barely missing the creature. The sports car bumped up onto the curb, and before Jay could get it back under control, it plowed into a light pole and mailbox, sending letters spraying into the hot air like snowflakes.

The air bags on both sides instantly inflated, saving both Jay and Scott's lives. But before either of them had a chance to react, a clawed fist smashed through the driver's-side window and grabbed Jay.

Scott watched in shock as his companion was yanked like a toy through the window and smashed down onto the hood of the car. A moment later the creature had cut off Jay's head and held it up to the sky, as if presenting tribute to some unseen god.

In the headlights of the car, Scott could see the shock frozen on Jay's face, the sudden meeting with death in his eyes. It was not a look Scott would soon forget.

If he lived long enough to have time to remember anything. He didn't know if it was better to get out of the car, or to try to hide inside. He was no match for that creature, and he didn't think the car would move.

Suddenly, the street in front of Scott lit up. Through the glare he could see army humvees and a half-dozen men, all heavily armed, facing the monster.

One man stood in the rear of the lead vehicle. He was holding an antitank missile launcher. "You just bagged your last trophy," he said. "Now it's my turn."

The man fired just as the creature in front of Scott jumped, Jay's head held tightly in its hand.

The missile cleared the hood of Jay's car by inches, missing the creature and exploding in the building behind Scott. The force of the blast sent Jay's car rolling into the street. All Scott could do was hang on and hope the seat belt held. It did, and the car ended up on its wheels, facing the action.

The monster landed on its feet and, with a smooth move, an almost major-league-pitcher move, threw Jay's head at the humvee. Jay's face smashed into the windshield. The driver yanked the wheel hard sideways, rolling the vehicle and spilling the three men inside onto the concrete.

Then the creature, at impossible speed, turned and headed down the street.

"Kill that thing!" one soldier on the ground shouted as he rolled over and came up with his gun in hand.

A roar of machine-gun fire broke out, filling the canyon between the buildings with bone-jarring sound. Scott watched as the bullets tore up a nearby building, missing the creature as it leaped onto the roof and was gone.

"Hold your fire!" another voice shouted, and the intense noise stopped.

Scott couldn't believe it was over. He just sat there, stunned, a cut on his head bleeding down his cheek, the deflated air bag draped over his legs. The lights on Jay's car were still on, and one beam spotlighted Jay's head, sitting upright in the middle of the street. His nose was smashed slightly, and some teeth were missing, but it looked as if every hair was still in place.

Slowly Scott started to laugh, softly, to himself as the relief flooded over him. He was still laughing—or was he crying?—as two of the soldiers came over to help him out of the car.

18

My brother, the monster slayer, has received all the training a monster slayer can have. He has learned how to protect himself, how to guard others, and when to sacrifice others. As a child, he learned all the wisdom of our people, wisdom that he is finally putting to use.

But those in charge do not understand. They order my brother around as if they are riding a blindfolded pony through a forest at full speed while they are blindfolded also. Such action can bring only pain, both to the rider and the pony.

Three more humvees slid to a stop between the buildings of Agate, New Mexico. They carried the colonel and a dozen other men.

Too late.

They had arrived too late.

Private Chaney wondered if that were on purpose.

He stood, weapon to his shoulder, his gaze never moving from what had been the front of a small grocery store, now riddled with bullet holes. A hardware store beside the grocery had a huge hole in the front where Corporal Nakai had shot an antitank weapon, just missing the creature. Smoke drifted from the hole like blood from a wound.

As men poured out of the newly arrived vehicles, Chaney lowered his rifle, his hands shaking. That creature had really been something. It had arms and legs like a man, yet it clearly wasn't human. It had cleared that grocery store in a single leap, as if simply jumping over a rock.

And the creature had used a man's head as a weapon. In his entire life, Chaney would never forget the image of that head smashing into the windshield of the humvee. There was no doubt in his mind that they were all lucky to be alive.

He forced himself to take a few deep breaths of the warm desert air. Originally he was from Boston, where the air was thick. A comforting weight that wrapped around a person and held him like a blanket holds a baby. He loved that air, and as soon as his hitch was up, he was headed back to work in his uncle's shipping factory on the harbor. It wouldn't be much of a job, but it would be a hell of a lot better than chasing monsters around a desert at night.

The colonel climbed out of the second humvee and walked over to Major Lee. An aide followed closely behind. Lee was surveying the damage as if he had never seen anything like it before. And he probably hadn't: Chaney hadn't, that was for sure. He doubted many of the men had.

Corporal Nakai remained sitting in the middle of the street, staring at where the monster had gone, shaking his head from side to side. Nakai didn't look frightened like the rest of the men. He just looked pissed.

Chaney let out a sigh. He wasn't far from the colonel or the major, so he made sure the sigh was a small one.

"I see you encountered the target," the colonel said.

"Yes, sir," Major Lee said.

"I sure hope those buildings are evacuated. It's action like this that gets civilians killed."

"The target got one," Lee said, pointing at the wrecked car and the head on the nearby sidewalk. "We saved another."

The colonel turned to look. His lips tightened when he saw the head. Chaney had seen the other head, near that cold campfire, but it hadn't been the same as seeing a monster actuallly rip the head off a living human being. The guy hadn't even had time to scream.

The colonel opened his mouth, but before he could say anything, Major Lee turned to two men nearby. "You two help that man out of the car, get him evacuated. You men scout out those buildings for any civilian casualties." The major pointed at three others and then at the hole in the front of the hardware store. "Get some water on those small fires in there before we burn down the entire town."

The seven men sprang into action and Chaney

stepped closer, waiting for his instructions. It seemed for the moment there wouldn't be any.

The colonel stepped up in front of Major Lee. "Give me the rundown on what happened here."

It took the major just thirty seconds to cover the details of the fight with the creature. The colonel clasped his hands behind his back and listened. Once he glanced at Nakai, who was still staring in the distance like a child who was waiting for his father to come home.

"It seems like Nakai underestimated this thing," the colonel said almost under his breath.

But apparently Lee caught the sentence, just as Chaney had. "Yes, sir. I was well aware of that only a few moments before, sir."

The colonel pivoted slightly and faced his aide. "Get me thirty more men airlifted in here, full battle gear, ready for night action. And I'm going to set up a field camp right here on this street."

"Yes, sir," the aide said, spun, and headed for the humvee.

The colonel turned back to Major Lee. "I want you and three others to figure out which direction this creature headed, but don't follow until I give the word. We're going after this thing with enough men to make sure we stop it."

"Understand, sir," Major Lee said. He turned. "Nakai, Mayhew, and Chaney, come with me."

Chaney started at the sound of his own name. He had been expecting an order, but not one that had him alongside Major Lee. Chaney was so surprised, he almost missed the colonel's next sentence.

"Not Nakai," the colonel said. "I want him here, with me, for the moment."

The major only nodded, then shouted, "Corales, you're with me."

Chaney again forced himself to take deep breaths of the thin air. He could feel the fear in his stomach pounding upward, wanting to get out. But somehow he forced it back down. Lee tossed them all industrial-strength flashlights. They had more lights in their gear, but when the major handed out specific lighting, you used it. The major just held his, without turning it on, and the others did the same. Lee gave them the signal, and they all fell in beside him as they headed toward the destroyed hardware store.

Chaney peered at it. The blast from the missile launcher had ruined the facade. Inside, the automatic fluorescents still glowed, showing debris all over the floor. Nuts, bolts, nails were scattered across the tile like spilled rice.

The buildings next to it also took damage, but not as much. The bullet holes would probably show up better in the daylight.

And then, because he couldn't help it, he looked up.

Part of him had hoped that the buildings were shorter than normal, that the creature had topped them because they were easy to jump over. But they weren't. No human could jump over them in a single bound. Not without jets attached to his feet.

The major turned down a side street. Chaney followed, glad to be beyond the destruction. The litter that covered the town was still present here, but there was no more dirt on this side street than there was in the back alleys of South Boston.

That soothed him just enough.

The desert was surprisingly close. One moment Lee, Chaney, and the others were in Agate. The next, they were in the desert. There were still scattered buildings, but very few. Outside one was a dog chain, with a dog collar at the end of it. Chaney didn't get close enough to see if there was any blood.

Lee switched on his flashlight and pointed it at the ground. The others did the same. The monster had to land somewhere, and wherever that was, he would leave a trail.

It took Major Lee and Chaney less than five minutes to pick up the creature's tracks. They were large and had ridges. Boots. The thing wore boots. Somehow, even though Chaney had seen it and its armor, he had thought that armor a part of the creature, just like an ant's armor was part of its body. The idea that this thing could remove its protection made it just a bit too intelligent for Chaney. He didn't mind fighting. In fact, he had itched for it just a few months before. But he really didn't want to fight something that was smart, ruthless, and unpredictable.

Chaney's light caught something green beside the footprints. Drops, like blood drops. He pointed his light at it, and Lee nodded.

"It's hurt," Lee said.

Maybe Nakai's blast had hurt it, or even one of Chaney's shots had found its mark. For some reason that calmed Chaney's nerves a little. If the creature could bleed, they stood a chance against it.

Lee shut off his flashlight. The others did the same. They stood for a moment in the dark. Chaney's heart was pounding. He felt curiously vulnerable, as though even the stars had eyes.

"Night goggles," Major Lee ordered as he snapped his into place. As he did, he checked his rifle, making sure he had a full clip.

Chaney did the same, managing to keep his hands from shaking too badly.

"We're only going along this trail for a few hundred yards," Major Lee said. "We want to make sure it didn't double back into the town. Chaney, go twenty meters to the left, Mayhew, twenty to the right. Corales, you and I will stay on the trail."

Without a word the four split up, moving off through the desert like ghosts. The night goggles lit up the desert, giving everything a flat green tint. Chaney had trained a number of times in the goggles, but always hated it. The last thing he wanted was to get into a fight with them on. But in the dark, it was better to have them than not to have them.

He moved right, away from the major, alternately watching the ground and the horizon ahead.

Chaney found his path moving him along the right side of a ridge as Major Lee and Corales followed the creature's trail up a ravine. Within fifty paces he couldn't see the other men and he had to force himself to stay calm and breathe the warm night air. Yet even focusing on that, he found himself holding his breath and listening.

After about two hundred paces along the ridge, he started across a flat, sandy area. In front of him was a shallow puddle of the monster's green blood. Instantly Chaney scanned both left and right, his finger on the trigger ready to open fire.

Nothing but the clear desert night greeted him.

"Chaney, the trail is headed your way," Major Lee's voice echoed through the night air.

Chaney cursed silently. They hadn't said they would be quiet, but he had assumed they would. If the thing was nearby, it had to hear them.

Nonetheless, the major expected an answer.

"I found the trail, sir," Chaney managed to yell back.

Suddenly the creature seemed to spring from the desert sand like a snake from a pit, towering over the private. Under the helmet Chaney could see razor-sharp teeth, and thick strands of hair.

The suddenness of it froze him in his tracks, his gun across his waist. He was looking up at a creature at least seven feet tall.

The creature reached out with one clawed hand and yanked the weapon from Chaney's grasp like a parent taking away a toy from a child. The motion snapped Chaney forward, toward the monster, into the thick smell of death that now filled the night air.

Chaney opened his mouth to scream. He had never felt so much terror in his life. He was going to die, and he wasn't ready. But at the hands of this creature, he had no choice.

The last thing he clearly saw was the creature's mouth saliva-dripping. Then, with one swipe, the creature severed Chaney's head, and his body bounced on the sand.

The predator held Chaney's head by its night goggles and raised its other fist in silent triumph. Then it attached the head to the rest of its trophies, and continued its hunt in the dark.

19

My brother has learned of monsters, monster slayers, and tradition, but he has not yet recognized himself as part of the legend. And he is running out of time.

Grandfather feels my brother must be reminded again. He must understand his place.

The small town of Agate was almost completely dark. Except for the streetlights, and the store lighting that was still on automatically, the place looked like a ghost town. Which, Nakai supposed, it was.

Nakai looked over his shoulder at a place where he had spent a lot of time. He knew that most of the people had left, but he also knew it was the way of things that a lot of people would stay. If he went into some of these old, familiar buildings, how many bodies would he find? How many more of his friends would he see, ripped and shredded by a crea-

ture that he would never have believed could exist a
week before?

Nakai made himself turn back to the colonel. He
stood at ease, waiting for the colonel to finish with
assignments. He had been waiting for some time
now. The colonel had called him aside especially,
and Nakai was not pleased about it. He had felt that
he belonged with Major Lee, in the desert, finding
the tracks of the creature. Yet the colonel had
stopped that order for a reason Nakai had yet to understand. With luck, the understanding would come
soon. It would be better not to let the trail of the
creature grow too cold.

Nakai still wasn't quite sure how the creature
got past him. Even knowing that the thing was powerful hadn't been enough; Nakai had overestimated
his own abilities, his own strengths. He had thought
it would take a single concentrated attack to bring
the thing down.

He was wrong.

He needed to focus, to come up with a better
plan. And he wasn't sure how to do that. He had a
feeling, though, that the colonel's plan was too or-
derly, too structured. This creature, for all its mon-
strous looks, had courage and intelligence. It had
outsmarted humans at every turn, almost as if it had
known what to expect.

"Corporal," the colonel said, turning to Nakai,
almost as an afterthought, "you and Tilden patrol
the town to the west."

The colonel started to turn away, but Nakai
stopped him. "Begging the colonel's pardon, sir," he
said.

The colonel turned, his eyes cold. Nakai suppressed a sigh. What was it about him that angered every officer he ever worked with? He had pointed this guy to the creature; he had set up the attack. Now the colonel was turning him away as if he had done something wrong. Nakai didn't care. He needed to be in the desert, going after that creature.

"Shouldn't I," Nakai continued, "be helping track the monster?"

"No, son," the colonel said, "you shouldn't." He took a deep breath and his face softened slightly. "I imagine you lost quite a few friends when your base was destroyed. Firing that missile into that building lets me understand that you want revenge just a little too much for all our good. It's understandable, but it's my policy to have men with personal vendettas removed from active duty."

The colonel took a step closer, and softened his voice even more so that the others couldn't hear. "I can't remove you from duty, son. Hell, you've done a lot for us. Getting us this close to the menace is medal country, in my opinion. But now I've got to stop you from ruining your own good work. I want you here, in town with me. Understood?"

Nakai didn't understand. He started to object, but he could see in the colonel's eyes that to do so would only make things worse. "Yes, sir," he said.

"Good," the colonel said. "Now, you and Tilden take up your positions. We don't know if that thing is going to circle back or not."

It was a bit of a gift, a way of saying that Nakai's job wasn't as unimportant as it seemed. But both men knew it wasn't true. That monster was done with Agate. It was looking for fresh blood.

Nakai managed not to say another word as he

saluted, snapped around, and headed west down the main street. Private Tilden dropped in beside him.

They walked the length of the main part of town in silence. Agate was empty, completely empty. Nakai had always wondered why people stayed in this godforsaken place, but now that they were gone, he felt bad, almost as if he personally had suffered a loss. He hadn't realized he was so attached to this place.

When they reached the abandoned railway warehouse that marked the edge of this part of town, Tilden spoke. Nakai, who had been lost in his own thoughts, had to turn, frown, and concentrate.

"What?" he asked.

Tilden smiled. "I was just saying you shouldn't take it so bad, Corporal. After all, you led us to that thing. You did your duty."

Nakai rolled his eyes, glad that Tilden couldn't see their expression in the darkness. Why was it that every time he had a setback, people told him he had done enough? His duty was the last thing at the moment he cared about. All he wanted to do was stop that monster.

"Let Major Lee and his boys do the rest," Tilden said. "I hear the colonel is flying in Major Amblin and his elite combat unit to go after the final kill."

"Great," was all Nakai could say. He jumped up on the loading dock, the old wood creaking under his feet. He scanned the surrounding area, finding exactly what he had expected: nothing. The night was still warm and the streetlights cast long shadows along the road. Just paces from where they stood, the desert stretched off into the distance, black under the star-filled night sky. The darkness was like an invitation. He could easily move out into that blackness and disappear. But he couldn't, because he would have to live with himself.

"Say," Tilden said, climbing up on the dock, "isn't Nakai a Navajo name?"

"Yeah," Nakai said, still scanning the darkness.

"Finally, a red brother," Tilden said.

"What?" Nakai turned to face the other man.

"Well, not exactly brothers," Tilden said, laughing at Nakai's fierce expression. "I'm Zuni."

Nakai nodded, relaxing a little. "My girlfriend's Zuni."

"Small world," Tilden said. "For Natives anyway."

"Yeah." Nakai held his rifle across his chest and leaned against the rough wood of the old warehouse, facing out over the desert.

"Not many of us in the army," Tilden went on. "Though that's no surprise. My dad hit the roof when I told him I was joining up. How'd your folks take it?"

"I was raised by my grandfather," Nakai said.

"Damn, that must have been worse." Tilden shook his head. "Older folks really don't understand."

Nakai nodded, looking off into the darkness, remembering the day he had told his grandfather he was joining the army. It was three years before, almost exactly to the day.

The day had been hot, even for the desert. Grandfather had been in his medicine tent. The temperature inside had to be ten degrees hotter than outside, but Grandfather didn't seem to notice. The

old man never seemed to notice either the heat of
the summer or the bitter cold of the winter.

Nakai had ducked inside, standing for a moment
with his back to the entrance, letting his eyes adjust
to the dark. Grandfather was sitting on the floor, a
drawing in the dirt in front of him. By Nakai's tribe,
Grandfather was considered *Yataali*, the medicine
man. He supposedly had great power, but Nakai had
never seen any of it actually help them.

"Grandfather," Nakai had said. "I have something to tell you. It's important."

"And I would like to tell you something,"
Grandfather replied. "Do you see this figure here?"
He pointed at a figure inside a triangle inside a larger
circle.

Nakai only nodded. He was familiar with the
drawing. It was the symbolic drawing of *Nayenezgani*,
the monster slayer. Nakai had seen the drawing
hundreds of times.

Grandfather pointed to another drawing in the
larger circle. "*Tobadjischini*, another of the hero
twins," he said. "*Nayenezgani's* twin brother. They
both play an important part in the night way."

Nakai had heard it all before. "Grandfather,
please, I must tell you something."

But Grandfather seemed to ignore him. "Without both twins, the evil cannot be banished. One
must distract the monster while the other kills it."

Nakai shook his head and decided to just press
on. "Grandfather, before I went down to the recruit-
ment office, I gave a lot of thought to what you said,
you know, about how being Navajo wasn't just in
your blood, but in your heart and the way you
acted."

Grandfather simply chanted softly over the drawing.

"I just want you to know," Nakai continued, "that no matter what you think, in my heart I will always be Navajo."

"I am *Yataali*," Grandfather said. "My people need my help to fight the evil, just as I need the help of the hero twins. *Nayenezgani* must help me or none of us will succeed."

"Grandfather," Nakai said, his voice almost pleading. "Please stop and listen to me. I know what you are saying. I have heard it before. I understand."

His grandfather, for the first time, looked up at Nakai, deep knowledge shining through his dark eyes. And in a very firm voice he said, "Do you, Grandson? Do you really know it, in your heart, as well as your head?"

And that was how it ended. Nakai had no answer. He had left the next day for boot camp and three weeks later his grandfather had died, sitting above the drawing of *Nayenezgani*.

20

Monsters, such as this one, are rare. They exist to keep us humble, to remind us that we are not the greatest creatures in the universe. They also exist to remind us of the relationship between predator and prey.

Without prey, the predator is nothing. When our people roamed freely, we blessed the spirit of our prey. We knew that without the prey, we would be nothing. We would not have clothing, or homes, or food.

We have lost our connection to our prey. We no longer understand the relationships that have kept us alive for all those centuries.

By losing touch with our prey, we have forgotten how to be predators.

We have forgotten how to survive.

Major Lee adjusted his night goggles. The damn things always made him slightly dizzy, something he didn't dare confess out loud. He figured it was because they reproduced the world in ways that were not natural. The desert didn't look like a night desert. It looked faintly grayish green, with all the details highlighted.

All the details, including the creature's bloody trail.

Private Corales stood beside Lee, holding his M-16 at the ready. Corales didn't seem disturbed by the night goggles. In fact, he was the one who had spotted the change in the creature's direction.

It veered to the right. Carefully, silently, Lee and Corales followed the trail to the top of a ridge. Lee felt the hair rise on the back of his neck. He'd been feeling like something was wrong, something was off.

He was feeling as if this part of the plan wasn't going well.

He kept telling himself it was because the attack in the town had gone badly. To let a civilian die—well, Lee would be lucky if he didn't have some music to face on that one. And then the damn creature got away.

Corales glanced at Lee as if he were expecting something. Lee was expecting something, and it wasn't coming. He had called to Private Chaney, to let him know about the change in the trail's direction, and Chaney had responded that he found it.

Then he had said nothing more.

Now, Chaney might be taking simple precautions. Even though Lee hadn't commanded silence, they all knew this creature was out there. Still, Chaney should have reported which direction he was going in.

Unless the direction was so damn obvious no one could miss it.

If that were the case, Chaney should have waited. No one in the team should have gone far from the others. Not alone.

That was basic tracking. Lee had trained Chaney himself. Lee remembered teaching that.

Lee shouted one more time. "Chaney. Report."

His order echoed through the night and died off in the warm breeze.

"Spread out," Lee said to Corales. "I want to go over that hill apart, just in case."

Corales nodded and went left about ten steps, stopping behind a small rock. Major Lee nodded and turned around, shouting back the thirty meters to Mayhew on the opposite ridge. "Move to our right and cover our flank."

Mayhew signaled that he had heard.

Lee glanced at Corales. "Ready, Private?"

"As ready as I'll ever be," Corales answered.

"Now," Lee said.

Together they went over the slight ridge, both moving parallel to the creature's tracks. No more than a few meters in front of them, just beyond the crest, was Chaney's body, his head severed, his gun missing.

"Damn it all to hell," Lee said softly as they both stopped and crouched, scanning the desert night for anything moving.

Nothing was.

Somehow that creature had killed Chaney without a sound, then disappeared into the night again. But how? And where was it now?

Before Major Lee could even move, his question

was answered. To their right the desert silence was shattered by the rapid fire of an assault rifle.

Both Corales and Lee dove for cover, coming up facing the sound of fire, guns at ready.

Mayhew screamed in agony, the cry echoing over the final sounds of gunfire like a haunting note.

Then again the desert was silent.

"Shit! Shit! Shit!" Lee said to himself. Then he called, "Mayhew, report!"

His words echoed and died.

"Mayhew, report!" Lee shouted louder.

Nothing.

"Shit!" Lee said again. Then with a wave to Corales, he motioned that they move up. More than anything he wanted to retreat, but until he discovered what had happened to Mayhew, he wasn't going anywhere.

Slowly, moving as carefully as they could through the brush and rock, they stalked toward Mayhew's position. No sound, no attacking fire greeted them. Nothing but the darkness and the desert breeze. And to Lee, the silence was worse than gunfire. At least with an attack, he knew what he was facing. At the moment he had no idea.

Finally, after what seemed like an eternity, but was less than a minute in real time, they reached Mayhew's body. He had been riddled point-blank by an M-16. Most of his middle had been blown into dripping blobs of flesh and intestines on the brush behind him.

Killed by Chaney's gun. The creature had done that on purpose, toying with them, letting them know that *it* knew that they were nearby.

Corales gagged, but held his dinner.

Lee moved slowly to the top of the ridge, scanning the area. From the looks of it, the creature had headed straight off into the desert, toward the volcanic ridgeline ten miles away. If it got into those rocks, not even Nakai could track it.

If it didn't, it was planning something. Lee gripped his gun tightly and searched the darkness, but saw nothing. For the first time he understood their disadvantage.

The creature, in using the M-16, had told them that it understood their weapons. It had weapons of its own, which it used with impunity. But by taking one of their weapons and turning it against their own man, it was sending a message.

It knew how they thought.

And they knew nothing about it.

The idea sent a chill through Lee. He took a deep breath to calm himself, then turned to Corales. "You all right?"

Corales nodded, his face a strange greenish color when viewed through the night goggles. Lee suspected that Corales was also that green when viewed without the night goggles.

"Good," he said. "Let's head back. We got to tell the colonel it's time we stopped playing army and kill this thing."

"Yeah," Corales said. "Before it kills us."

Lee clapped Corales on the back. He didn't agree, at least not verbally. He didn't have to.

After one more glance at the desert, the men turned and headed quickly toward the lights of the nearby town.

21

My grandfather tells me that my brother might finally understand his place in the way of things. My grandfather tells me the time is yet to come. He is a powerful Yataali. I must believe him. I must remain at my brother's side until the time is right for him to slay the monster.

"Hey, Corporal." Tilden's voice broke into Nakai's memory of the last time he had seen his grandfather alive. "Can you hear me there?"

"I'm sorry," Nakai said, scanning the desert, seeing nothing. "Just drifted off there for a second. Been a long day."

"Yeah," Tilden said. "It has at that."

They stood in silence for a moment. Nothing moved around them, and no noise came from the center of town. A warm wind drifted off the desert, bringing nothing but normal smells to Nakai. The creature wasn't out there in this direction, that much was for sure. And guarding this end of town was a waste of time. It was simply a way to keep him out of the kill.

Nakai shifted his feet, and the loading dock creaked beneath him. He wondered how secure it was. The abandoned warehouse had been old when he first came to Agate.

He leaned his head against the rough wood and tried to peer deeper into the desert. The silence was eerie. The shadows from the town's lights were right, but the background noise was all wrong. At this time of night, he should have heard more than one car rev its motor as it was about to head onto the straight desert road. The music from Ben's Saloon would have carried this far as well, provided it was a weekend and Ben had hired a band—or what passed for a band in Agate. And if there was no music, there would at least be conversation: loud drunken conversation, usually about pool, usually spilling into the roadway.

There was nothing.

Nothing except Tilden breathing softly beside him. Shouldn't the kid be walking point at least?

"You know," Tilden said, breaking the silence. He had amazing timing. Nakai was about to tell him to scout a bit. "They mentioned at the briefing that this creature had some sort of deadly ray that killed people."

"Yeah," Nakai said. Instantly the image of the blue flash cutting through Dietl rose in his mind. He'd have that memory for the rest of his life, and it would come at the most inconvenient moments. Damnation, he wished he could once remember how Dietl had been when he was alive. "The weapon fired like blue lightning. I was the one who told them about it."

"Wonder why the creature didn't use it when *we* attacked it," Tilden said. "Think its ray gun might be broken or something?"

Nakai froze in place. He had missed that. How had he missed that?

"Damn," he whispered. The truth of the situation was dawning on him. "I wonder why I didn't think of that."

"What?" Tilden asked.

"You stay on post," Nakai said. "I've got to report to the colonel on this."

"But—"

Without waiting for Tilden to finish, Nakai headed off at a run toward the center of town. It didn't take him very long to get there.

The colonel's men had set up a large tent against the back of one building. A guard patrolled the top of the building and two more stood post on corners. Inside the tent, Nakai could see the colonel sitting at a table, studying a map.

Nakai slowed to a walk when he reached the sentry positions. Outside the edge of the open tent flat, he stopped and saluted. "Colonel, sir."

The colonel glanced up, frowning. "What is it, Corporal?" His voice was tired and sounded annoyed.

"Begging the colonel's pardon for the interruption, but I've got to talk with you, sir."

The colonel motioned for Nakai to come in, but didn't offer him one of the open chairs. Instead he went back to studying the map.

The colonel had really changed his mind about Nakai. Or was he afraid of him? Afraid of a man who had come through the desert on his own, who had survived meeting that creature, not once, but three times.

"Sir," Nakai said. "I believe the creature has a camp."

The colonel looked up. "A camp?"

"Yes, sir," Nakai said. "When this creature killed Dietl, it was with a blue bolt of some kind or another. And when I came upon the creature in the desert, it fired on the cat using the same weapon. Yet tonight it didn't fire on us."

The colonel studied Nakai. "Do you believe you have some special understanding of this creature, Nakai?"

"Yes, sir."

The colonel brought his head back, as if he were surprised.

Nakai held out his hands. He would make or break his own argument here. Now. "I've had more time to study it, sir, than anyone else has. And I've been thinking about its patterns. It acts like a hunter."

"A hunter?"

Nakai nodded. "It has traveled here, alone, and it hides. It stalks its prey, and it is very careful to take souvenirs. It carries those souvenirs with it."

"That doesn't mean it's a hunter, Nakai," the colonel said. "Tourists carry souvenirs."

"That's my point, sir. If you were big-game hunting in Africa, wouldn't you make sure you kept a scrap of everything you bagged—a tooth, an antler, something—even if you ate the creature?"

The colonel kicked out a chair and sighed. "You certainly make a good argument, Nakai. Have a seat."

Nakai sat down.

"A hunter."

"Yes, sir. It doubles back. It watches us—its prey. It uses weapons in very precise ways, and when it's outnumbered, it runs."

"That seems only logical," the colonel said.

"And remember, it seems to have some kind of camouflage ability." Nakai cleared his throat, uncomfortable with this next. "And when it has time, it dresses its kill like we would dress a dear."

The colonel slid the map toward Nakai. "So you think it has a camp."

"Yes, sir." Nakai's heart was pounding. He had convinced the colonel to respect him again. That was critical. Once he had the man's full respect, he would request a return to duty. Real duty. That meant going after the creature.

"A camp," the colonel mused. "Well, why not? If it can fly a craft, it can build a camp." Then his eyes narrowed. "But we are making assumptions here. Just because the creature didn't fire doesn't mean it wasn't carrying its weapons."

"True," Nakai said. "But there's another detail I missed this morning that I should have seen. The creature left a trail from the site where he killed the big cat toward the north, and then back again. He obviously went into those lava flows and returned, for some reason. I didn't give it much thought, since they were older tracks, but if his camp is in those lava rocks, he might have left weapons and supplies there, before he blew up his ship in Cole."

"Setting out from a camp without a weapon doesn't make much sense," the colonel said, thinking aloud. He shook his head slowly. "But then, from what I've seen of this creature, it doesn't need a weapon most of the time."

"Yes, sir," Nakai said. Now was his chance. "I just might be able to track it back to its camp if you give me a chance."

"Well, . . ." The Colonel sat back and thought for a moment. He never finished his sentence. Suddenly the sound of gunfire echoed over the town, coming clearly from the north side, where Major Lee had gone.

Where the creature had gone.

Nakai was off his chair instantly, his rifle ready. The colonel stood and moved around to stand beside him, both of them listening.

"Damn it," the colonel said. "I told them not to engage the creature until we had the right men and equipment here."

"Maybe they didn't have a choice, sir," Nakai said. The creature rarely gave anyone a choice.

The colonel nodded.

Silence covered the town as everyone waited. Nakai admired the colonel for not sending more men to investigate at once. A lesser leader would have done just that, and possibly sent even more men to their deaths. Instead the colonel stood and waited.

Within a minute of the gunshots, Major Lee and Private Corales came running at full speed around the corner of the destroyed hardware store.

The major ran directly up to the colonel and snapped off a salute, "Sir," he said, breathless and sweating, the dirt forming streaks on his sunburned skin. "Chaney and Mayhew are dead."

"Damn it all," the colonel said. He took a deep breath, obviously upset at the news. "What happened?"

"The creature must have ambushed Chaney," Major Lee said, "then took his gun. It killed Mayhew with Chaney's rifle while making its escape. It seems to be headed directly north."

"Toward the lava fields and its camp," Nakai said.

"It would seem that way," the colonel said, glancing at Nakai, then turning back to Major Lee. "Suggestions, Major?"

"Sir," Lee said, "I think we should bring in everything we can bring in, before it reaches those lava fields. If it gets in there, we'll never get it out."

The colonel nodded. He turned and moved back into the tent, dropping down into his chair. "I agree," he said. "I've got an elite commando unit coming in on a chopper, escorted by a gunship. They'll be here within an hour's time."

Major Lee nodded and smiled. "Good."

Nakai also agreed with Lee. Army commando units consisted of fourteen of the best-trained fighters in the world, and a helicopter gunship had more firepower than almost anything aloft. Against one creature, they might get the job done.

"But let's not take any chances," the colonel said. "Major, I want you to round up all the men around town, leaving two to stay with the dead. Corporal Nakai?"

Nakai, who had been listening intently, snapped to attention. If the colonel stuck him with guarding bodies, he'd go over the wall. He wasn't pulling guard duty at a time like this. Not for any reason. "Yes, sir."

"Think you can track that thing through the desert at night?"

"Yes, sir," Nakai said, smiling.

"Good," the colonel said. "Major Lee, have the humvees ready to go in five minutes. We're going to drive that creature right into the commandos and kill the damn thing."

Nakai could only smile. Finally, the army was doing as he had hoped, working smart and working together. Just maybe, if they were lucky, they'd bag that creature tonight.

If they weren't lucky, a lot of men were going to die.

22

The story of the twins, of Nayenezgani, *has been told from father to son for generations. The center of the story concerns the monster's power. A monster must show its true power before its defeat can be honored in a story. Killing a field mouse is easy. Killing a cougar is hard. Killing this monster, this creature, is almost impossible.*

That is the task of the monster slayer; doing the impossible.

This monster has destroyed an entire army base full of people, and killed dozens more. But it has not yet shown its true power. I fear that when my brother understands this, he will turn away.

The monster slayer must remain forever strong. My brother has never been good at doing anything for long periods of time. Especially things that are difficult.

. . .

It didn't take long to get the troop organized. Nakai was amazed at how efficiently the colonel's units ran.

Within ten minutes of receiving the order, Major Lee and Corporal Nakai led the twenty-six men out into the desert, leaving the buildings and lights of Agate behind. Nakai was relieved to get out of there. He needed to go after this monster. He felt that every second wasted was another second that gave the creature an advantage.

He felt it had enough advantages already.

The colonel rode in one of two vehicles to the rear of the group. The humvees were going to have rough going at times, and the colonel had given orders for Nakai and Major Lee not to worry about the vehicles keeping up. They would find a way.

Major Lee had agreed, but had asked respectfully that the colonel have two soldiers in each humvee, plus the drivers. The colonel agreed. That left nineteen men on foot.

The first destinations were the bodies. They weren't that far apart. Nakai stopped long enough at each to note if there were any differences from the previous kills, and to allow Major Lee to dispatch two of the men to move the bodies back to town.

At Chaney's body, Nakai learned nothing new. The creature had acted just as Nakai had thought it would act: a quick kill and a rapid beheading.

It was Mayhew that made him stop. The use of the M-16 bothered him. Lee saw the weapon's use as a message. Nakai agreed with that. But weapons were particular things: each culture had traditions and ways of using them. This creature had picked up the gun and used it within minutes.

Nakai had seen the creature's weapon fire, and knew he could no longer use it. But the creature had figured out the army's weapon of choice. Either the creature was a quick study or it was already familiar with the weapon when it came to New Mexico.

Nakai wagered the creature was already familiar with it.

There were a lot of things Nakai hadn't said to the colonel, things that weren't really relevant to their pursuit of this creature. But it bothered him that the creature had known where to come. This desert, complete with army base, was like a game preserve. There were humans here, protected yes, but within structured limits. There was also a perfect place to make camp. Nakai suspected this creature hadn't happened upon this place; he suspected the creature had come here purposely.

All Nakai could do at this time was thank every god he could think of that the creature seemed to have come alone.

Now, as the unit strode into the desert, their force was down to seventeen soldiers on foot and six in the two humvees, plus the colonel. Nakai only hoped they wouldn't catch up to the creature before the commandos were in position. He doubted they would. The creature that they attacked in Agate also didn't use its invisibility power as it had when Dietl was killed. Nakai would bet almost anything that that power was contained in a part of its armor left in its camp in the lava rocks.

The creature's tracks were easy to follow, even in the desert night. It was making no attempt to cover its trail, but simply striding at a steady pace directly north, toward the lava fields.

Major Lee ordered all the men to use their night goggles, but Nakai ignored the order. He had lived in the nights of this desert his entire life. The sky was clear, the stars out. To him, the desert was a clear as daylight.

Nakai glanced around. Tilden also had his night goggles on his head, unused. Nakai nodded to him and Tilden nodded back. They both felt they carried the responsibility of getting this troop through the desert. This was their desert, their backyard. They knew it and loved it. It was the way of both their peoples.

Nakai turned toward the desert and set a fast pace, walking beside the creature's tracks, striding as fast as he safely could through the desert brush and rocks.

Tilden paced him to his right, staying just behind, but moving as surely as Nakai.

From what Nakai could tell, the creature had approximately a twenty-minute head start on them. And judging from the length of its stride, it would be able to move faster than they could. But even at its fastest pace, the creature wouldn't reach the lava fields before the commandos were in place.

It bothered him that the monster made no attempt to hide its tracks. Another signal? Or a trap?

Nakai wanted to be prepared for both.

Around and behind him the seventeen soldiers on foot sounded more like a buffalo stampede then a night search. At the pace Nakai was setting, there was no way anyone but a trained scout could move through this desert brush at night without making noise. Nakai could and Tilden could. But the other fifteen soldiers, in full gear, followed by two humvees scattering rock and crashing through brush, could more than likely be heard for miles, a clear rumble echoing under the stars like an unseen thunderstorm in a far-distant mountain range.

That was exactly what Nakai wanted. He wanted that creature to know they were right behind it. With luck, it would be paying more attention to them than to its path ahead, and the commandos would have open shots.

Now Nakai only needed to make sure the creature didn't stop and take them on first.

After five minutes, when it became evident that the creature wasn't altering its path, Nakai slowed for a moment, just long enough to let Major Lee catch up with him.

"Sir," Nakai said. "I think I need to move out ahead, with only one man thirty meters behind me, and another thirty behind him. I would like the main group to remain thirty behind the last man."

"In case the creature sets a trap?" Lee said.

"Yes," Nakai said.

Lee nodded. "Do it."

"Put Private Tilden behind me," Nakai said. "He's Zuni and used to this desert."

Again Major Lee nodded. Then he stopped and held up his hand for all the men to stop.

Nakai just kept moving ahead without breaking stride. Behind him he heard the major say, "Tilden, follow Corporal Nakai. Make sure you stay thirty meters behind him and ready."

"Yes, sir," Tilden said.

After thirty paces, Nakai glanced around. In the darkness he could see Tilden step out after him. He couldn't hear him. Tilden was just as silent as Nakai expected him to be. Nakai nodded, then returned his attention to the task at hand: following the creature's trail in the dark desert and making sure the creature wasn't stopped ahead, waiting to ambush him. Ten more minutes and the commandos would be in position ahead, flanked along the edge of the lava field, hiding, waiting for the creature to be driven right into them.

This plan was so simple. If only it worked.

Behind him the entire troop started up again, filling the desert quiet with the sound of cracking brush, rattling rock, and engines.

Nakai smiled to himself. It was a good sound, a comforting sound. For the first time in a long while he was glad he wasn't in the desert alone.

23

My brother, Nayenezgani, *the monster slayer, must slay the monster alone. He does not know this yet. Only I, his dead twin brother, can help him. He hopes to change the story of our ancestors, but he cannot do so. It is the way the story has been told. Our ancestors knew of the monster, knew of my brother. He cannot change the way of history any more than he can change the color of his skin.*

Two miles ahead the pitch-black ridgeline of the lava fields loomed above the desert floor. Centuries before, the area ahead had been teeming with life. Successive volcanic eruptions had coated the entire region with a ragged, black landscape of hardened lava, covering roughly two hundred square miles of northern New Mexico. The Spanish called the place El Malpais: "The Bad Country."

The Navajos had another name for it: *Ye'iitsoh*

Bedit Ninigheezh. Literally translated it meant: "Where big enemy god's blood clotted." Supposedly, in those black rocks, the twin of *Nayenezgani* distracted the monster while his brother took careful aim and pierced the giant's heart. The monster's blood flowed and eventually hardened into the black sea of rock.

Or so went the Navajo myth.

Nakai knew it well. His grandfather had brought him to this ridgeline for the first time when he was a small boy. They had stood in the twilight, and his grandfather had told him the myth. Nakai remembered the moment clearly: his grandfather was such an excellent storyteller that Nakai had thought he had seen the battle happening before him.

Now his memory was tainted. Now, when he saw the giant of the myth, he saw the talons and armor of the monster he was currently pursuing.

For the first time he was truly starting to understand what his grandfather had been telling him.

Nakai kept glancing up at the black ridgeline, looking for the creature, trying to catch a glimpse of the commando forces he knew were in position there. Of course he couldn't see them. If he could, they would be doing a very, very bad job. More than likely, the transport chopper had come in low from the north, escorted by the gunship, and dropped off the commandos under cover. Then, the gunship would have been hidden in a ravine, waiting to rise up from the black lava like death itself.

But still Nakai watched the ridgeline and kept moving. The last hour had gone quickly. The creature hadn't altered its course in the slightest, and from what Nakai could tell, it would be approaching those lava fields within the next few minutes if it hadn't altered its pace.

Now, the closer he got to that black ridge, the slower time moved.

Nakai kept his silent march forward, tracking the creature. Tilden stayed behind him, also moving silently ten paces off to the right of his track and thirty paces back. Nakai felt comfort that the other man was there.

He trusted Tilden. Tilden understood the desert. That counted for more than Nakai could say.

The rest of the troop lumbered along, obviously tired. Somehow the drivers of the two humvees had managed to keep up. Considering some of the desert they had crossed in the last hour, that was an amazing feat of driving skill and luck.

Now the ridgeline was less than a half-mile ahead. The creature had either stopped, or had slipped through the commandos, since no gunfire had broken the night. Nakai bet it had stopped.

Nakai reached a rock ledge and halted, crouching, looking over the desert remaining between him and the edge of the lava flow. It was a shallow valley, with a dry streambed running left to right. On his side was a natural rock outcropping, worn down almost to rubble by the winds and floods. On the opposite side of the shallow valley was the black edge of the lava flow. Somewhere in that shallow valley was the creature, Nakai was sure. But where and why it had stopped were other matters.

Nakai motioned for those behind him to halt, then turned back to face the valley again. With a final thrust of crackling brush and engines sputtering and clicking, the noise died off, leaving only the normal sounds of the desert. A moment later, silently, Tilden slipped in beside him, crouching as Nakai was doing.

Together they studied the area in front of them, watching for any movement, anything unusual at all. There was nothing. Not even the slight breeze brought Nakai the smell of the creature. Yet the tracks went on straight ahead, down over the edge of the valley, still unvarying, right into the bottom.

Nakai glanced around and motioned for Major Lee to join them. Lee moved up quietly, kneeling beside Nakai. The major was panting softly. The forced, high-speed march through the desert was obviously not something he was used to.

"Do you have an infrared scope?" Nakai whispered.

Major Lee nodded and opened a pouch on his side. He pulled out what looked to be a pair of binoculars, yet without lenses on the outside. Instead of looking through them as Nakai had figured he would do, the major handed them to Nakai, leaving his own night glasses in place.

Nakai brought the scope to his eyes and quickly adjusted it. Then he followed the tracks of the creature ahead until he found what he was looking for. The creature was crouched on a ledge about halfway up the lava slope, straight across from them. The creature seemed to be looking back in their direction.

Nakai scanned the lava ridge. He saw no evidence of the commandos.

He handed the scope back to the major. "It's straight ahead," he whispered. "Halfway up the slope."

The major flipped up his night goggles, then put the scope to his eyes. A moment later he whispered, "Got him."

Lee handed the scope back to Nakai, who slipped it to Tilden.

"Stay put until I give the order," Lee said, slipping his night goggles back into place. He moved, quickly and quietly, back the way he had come. He had to report to the colonel.

Nakai hoped the man would hurry. This was the second time he had seen the creature before it saw him, and the last time, the only thing that saved Nakai's life was the lucky appearance of that puma.

Nakai wanted this creature dead, and soon. The longer they waited, the better the creature's chances got.

"Any ideas how we're going to get it off that lava?" Tilden whispered, staring through the scope at the creature.

"We aren't," Nakai whispered back. "With luck, the commandos and the gunship will do it."

Behind him Nakai heard the movement of the men spreading out along the ridgeline, taking up positions facing the valley and the creature on the far edge. They were too far away to open fire, so clearly the colonel intended them all to storm the creature while the commandos and the chopper came in over the top of it. They were to be the diversion and backup.

The plan was risky, but it might work. Nakai hoped that none of the men around him got close enough to take a shot. If that happened, the plan had gone very, very wrong.

The noise around them died down as Tilden

handed Nakai back the scope. The creature, outlined by its heat and shape in the infrared, hadn't moved. It was just crouching there, black stone at its back.

Clearly it was waiting for the army to make the first move into an easily defended position. If nothing else, this creature knew the ways of war and fighting. Nakai would have picked a similar position if he had been pursued by a larger force. The problem was the creature didn't know about the helicopter gunship waiting just out of sight and earshot. No position on that rock face was defensible against that kind of firepower from the air.

The colonel and Major Lee joined Nakai and Tilden.

"We're ready to go in," the colonel said. "See any problems?"

"Yes," Nakai said. "That creature is defended and prepared. It knows about the ground troops."

"Just as we planned."

"But there's no way it could know about the gunship," Nakai said. "Let's just make sure it goes in first."

"I was planning on it, Corporal," the colonel said.

The colonel stood, forcing Lee, Nakai, and Tilden to do the same. "Move out, people," he said, loud enough for all the men to hear up and down the line. "Make some noise, but not too much."

Nakai moved left of the creature's trail; Tilden moved right as the rest of the men started down the shallow slope, kicking up rock and snapping brush and twigs.

It sounded like a cattle stampede. He couldn't

believe the amount of noise they were making, all seemingly without trying to do so.

Then ahead, right over the position of the creature, there was a humming sound that grew deeper and deeper, as if the entire earth was shaking. Nakai had heard that sound a number of times. It was the gunship emerging from the ravine.

"Goggles up!" the colonel shouted.

An instant later the night that had covered the valley became day as the gunship lit up the side of the lava rock and a half-dozen white flares exploded in the sky, turning the darkness into phosphorescent daylight.

Nakai could see the creature clearly now, crouched against the rock, looking up at the gunship. He wondered how it felt at that moment, knowing it was going to die very shortly. Maybe that wasn't what it was thinking at all.

Instantly, the gunship fired four rockets at the creature. Red streaks, like blood against the lit-up sky, shot from the helicopter and smashed into the creature's position, exploding with enough force for Nakai to feel it clear across the valley.

"That ought to take care of that problem," Major Lee said.

"I wouldn't be so sure, sir," Nakai said as they all kept moving forward. That creature had surprised him before. He had finally learned to take nothing about it for granted.

As he spoke, from out of the exploding rock where the creature had been hidden, something shot upward, catching the gunship squarely in the center.

The resulting explosion rocked Nakai and Tilden

and sent Major Lee tumbling over backward in the
desert dirt. Nakai covered his head quickly and
ducked, waiting for the intense explosive light to
clear, and any shrapnel. After a moment that
seemed to last forever, he stood.

And so did the creature, rearing up like a cornered bear, its back to the lava.

The gunship was a falling pile of burning metal.
Almost in slow motion it crashed into the rocks on
the valley floor just below the creature, and exploded again, filling the air with smoke and yellow
flame.

The commandos were now on rocks all around
the creature, firing at will. The creature staggered
backward, again caught by surprise as it was hit over
and over.

Suddenly the blue energy shot out from a
weapon mounted on the creature's shoulder. The
bolts looked like blue death, and they were aimed
directly at the commandos. The beams exploded on
contact. The power of that weapon was immense,
easily slicing through commandos who were in the
open.

Five of the commandos were cut down in the
first moments of the fight. The rest dove for cover.

Nakai shook his head. So much for the creature
leaving its weapons in a camp. Obviously this creature was far from unarmed. It just chose when to
use a weapon and when not to, as any good soldier
would do.

"Return fire!" the colonel shouted.

They were definitely in range now. Nakai and
Tilden both dropped to cover behind rocks, leveled
their rifles on rocks, and began firing. Both of them

chose to pull off single shots. Nakai figured the chance of hitting the creature at this range was much, much better with well-aimed fire. Clearly Tilden had the same thought.

Most of the other men down the line opened up with full automatic fire.

The sounds of the weapons echoed and doubled back, loud enough to do damage to any human ear. Nakai hoped that the noise bothered the creature, hoped that it struck some fear into the thing.

The creature dove for cover into the lava rocks, firing as it went.

One of the humvees exploded not far from Nakai, sending orange and red debris into the smoke-filled air. Beside it a man screamed and rolled in the dirt, trying to put out the gas fire engulfing him.

Nakai kept squeezing off shots through the smoke at the spot where the creature had hidden behind rocks. Dozens of other men on both sides of the canyon were firing, some in bursts, others, like Nakai, firing one shot at a time.

The creature leaped into view, firing rapidly with the blue-flamed weapon. A dozen explosions to Nakai's right shook the ground as men died, some screaming in pain, some making no more than the thick, wet sound as their insides were blown out.

The commandos on the rocks closer to the creature were taking even more of a beating. They were being picked off like ducks sitting on the shore of a pond. It seemed the creature never missed.

But the remaining men were scoring hits. Nakai could tell every time a bullet pounded into the creature, making it jerk backward. Its entire body couldn't be covered with armor. Some of those bullets had to be getting through, causing damage.

Nakai and Tilden kept pulling off shots, consistently, both of them finding their mark, but since they were firing singly, and were at a distance, the creature focused its firepower on the closer commandos, and the men down the line who were firing in long bursts.

Three more shots of blue death shot out.

Three more men died.

Then the monster started to move. With a quick bound, it was on top of the lava flow. Quickly, it fired a dozen more blasts, exploding rock and bodies with blue fire.

The second humvee exploded.

Six more commandos died.

Three more men in the valley were cut in half.

Then the creature was gone, vanished over the ridge into the black lava field.

The gunfire slowed and stopped. In the sky, small parachutes still held up the flares of white light, flooding the smoke and fire-filled valley with reality.

Death was everywhere.

Both Nakai and Tilden were slow to get up. They both kept their rifles aimed on the place where the creature had disappeared, just in case it wanted to come back and finish the job of killing them all. It had come close as it was.

Finally, Tilden said, "Shit."

Nakai pushed himself to his feet and shouldered his rifle. The creature wasn't coming back. It had won this battle. It didn't need to return.

Nakai looked around him. The flares slowly

drifted down and went out, leaving only the fires from the wrecked gunship and the two burning humvees to light the valley. Flickering yellow light that revealed broken weapons, and bodies, and blood.

"Major?" Tilden said, moving to where Major Lee lay, facedown. "Major?"

Nakai stood over him as Tilden rolled Lee over. His face was gone, blown off when a burst of blue flame had caught the right cheek. Only smoking, stinking, cauterized brains filled the area where Lee's face had been.

Tilden quickly stood and took a step back, forcing himself to breathe deeply. It was the image of nightmares.

Nakai did the same, and together they stood there and surveyed the carnage. Of the thirty-some soldiers and commandos who had gone into battle against one creature, fewer than ten remained. Beside one humvee, the colonel stood, shaking his head in complete disbelief. Nakai could almost read his thoughts.

It should have been enough.

If they had brought this much weaponry in on any human, no matter how well defended, the man would be dead.

They had wounded this thing, but they hadn't destroyed it.

Nakai suspected that they hadn't even come close.

The colonel wasn't moving yet. He looked stunned. Nakai knew how he felt. One creature had defeated this many well-trained troops, in conditions that favored the army, not the creature.

"What the hell is this thing?" Tilden asked.

"*Adikgashii*," Nakai said.

Tilden looked at him, his mouth open. "If that thing is *Adikgashii*," Tilden said. "Who is *Nayenezgani*?"

Nakai stared at the ridge where the creature had disappeared, then said softly, "I am."

24

My twin brother finally has admitted his destiny. He has learned the true nature of being Navajo. Grandfather is pleased. From the other side, it is easy to understand the ways of the living. Yet the living have such difficulty. Grandfather says that the process of understanding is the most important part of life. The value is in the learning, not in the result.

The rest of the night was like a long nightmare for Nakai. It took the remaining men over an hour to check the entire battlefield for wounded. There weren't any. It seemed that when that a blue ray hit a human, it killed him. Period. Nakai had never seen so many human body parts not attached to full bodies in all his life.

The stench was the worst part. Bodies in pieces had an odor all their own. Nakai dreaded dawn, and with it, the full power of the sun. Then the stench would be unbearable.

He had expected problems, but he hadn't expected this. He hadn't thought the creature would be this impossible to kill.

If it had taken this much effort to wound it, how much effort would it take to kill the creature?

He suspected he was going to find out.

After they found Major Lee's body, the colonel appointed Nakai as second in command. Nakai immediately posted guards at all four points on the perimeter of the valley. A single guard wouldn't be able to hold off the creature, but he might give the rest of them warning.

The remaining group completed the check of the bodies, and then reported the grim news to the colonel. He must have already suspected it, because he just nodded. The colonel was covered with as much blood and gore as the rest of them. He had been in the midst of that carnage, searching, with the others.

Nakai respected him for that.

After the group had made its report, the colonel had visibly gathered himself to give the next orders. All the radios were shot up, so the colonel asked for a volunteer to hike back to Agate to use the radios left there. Tilden raised his hand. Nakai thought him a good choice, since Tilden could move through the desert as well as Nakai. That meant Tilden would get to Agate quickly.

The colonel gave Tilden the message to send back to base: airlift in more troops. This time the colonel also requested tanks and more gunships. Then he told Tilden to tell the base to stand by for air strikes, another move Nakai knew was a good idea.

Tilden had been gone just under an hour, not quite long enough for him to reach Agate at full speed, when Nakai decided what he had to do. The day was still just a promise in the eastern sky, the oranges and reds leaching into the sky as though a giant god had spilled oil colors in water.

The light, thin as it was, fell on the destruction. The humvees were crumpled hunks of metal in the midst of a ruined landscape. Bodies, unmoved except to be checked for life, were sprawled where they fell. Guns sat upright in the dirt, or bent in half by the force of blows.

Nakai had never seen anything like it in his life.

He hoped not to see anything like it again.

Nakai turned his back on the devastation, and went to look for the colonel. The man had disappeared after giving Tilden his orders. Nakai hadn't seen him since.

It took Nakai a bit of searching before he spotted the colonel. He was sitting with two men, his back against a rock, waiting. He had a shocked, empty look in his eyes. The colonel had never been to the Gulf. Nakai remembered hearing that, but he hadn't realized that this was the man's first live combat situation, and the first time he had sent other men to their deaths. And it ended so badly. How he handled the next few hours would be a sign of his true value to the army.

"Sir," Nakai said, moving up and crouching next to the colonel.

"Yes, son?" the colonel said. His voice sounded the same. Only his eyes were different. Nakai doubted the colonel's eyes would ever be the same again.

"We need to find out where that creature went, sir."

The colonel nodded for a moment, then closed his eyes. Nakai could almost feel his reluctance to make another decision, to do anything that could result in such damage again.

Nakai held his breath, then the colonel looked at him. The strong man Nakai had met two nights before was still there. He was just in shock. "What do you suggest?"

"Let me see if I can track him in there. I should be able to get a bead on his camp and we can take it out from the air."

The colonel frowned. He was clearly beginning to think through the shock. "Can you track him over that rock?"

"I honestly don't know, sir," Nakai answered. "We hit him with enough firepower so that with luck he's bleeding. I can follow the blood trail, if there is one."

"He was bleeding before," the colonel said. "There should be a trail. That creature is strong, but nothing could have gotten out of there without some damage." He glanced at his watch. "You've got two hours before we're staged and ready to roll. If you're not back, we'll go anyway."

Nakai nodded. "I'll be back by then."

"No grandstanding, soldier," the colonel said as Nakai stood. "I want you back here alive. We've lost enough good men to this creature."

"I don't intend to die at the hands of that thing," Nakai said. "I'll be back."

"Good luck," the colonel said. He stood. Evidently the conversation had helped him regain his focus. He would step past his inner turmoil to do what he needed to in order to prepare for the attack.

Nakai had no inner turmoil at all to deal with. He was past it. He had seen this creature kill his friend Dietl. And then it had wiped out his entire base. He was far beyond the shock of it all. Now he was just tired and angry.

Five minutes later, without so much as a good-bye, he patted the northernmost guard on the shoulder and climbed up the lava flow. Nakai was loaded down with ammunition for his M-16. If he did run into the creature, he was going to get off a few shots before he died.

About halfway up the side of the lava flow was the ledge where the creature had taken cover and waited. The area was scarred almost white from the blast marks of the missile attack. That the creature had survived so much firepower was a miracle. Then, stepping onto the ledge, Nakai saw the reason.

The creature had chosen a perfect spot for defense. It wasn't just a ledge, but running back and to the right was a fairly deep cave, now filled with shattered rock, like pebbles of sand on a beach. Clearly the creature, seeing the rockets coming, had ducked back into cover, shielding itself from the brunt of the impact. Then, while the smoke was still thick, it had emerged and shot down the chopper.

"Smart," Nakai said. "Real smart."

Too smart. Every time he thought he had a bead on this creature, it proved that he had underestimated it. But there was one thing Nakai hadn't underestimated.

The creature was wounded.

Green blood was scattered all over the ledge.

The sight made Nakai smile. "So, you ugly bastard. We hurt you."

He glanced back over the shallow valley. The chopper was still burning slowly below him, sending up black smoke into the early-morning sky. The colonel and a few others were sitting, backs against the rock ledge on the far side. Every detail of the valley could be seen from here, including the burned and ripped bodies of dozens of soldiers. It was no wonder they took so many casualties. They had been like sitting ducks to a creature with the weapons it had.

Nakai shook his head in disgust and turned away, following the green spots up over the top of the ridge and onto the lava flow. At first sight, the flow was as flat and open as the desert. But on closer inspection, the black surface was scarred with deep ravines and moundlike hills. The black rock under Nakai's feet was mostly smooth, and in places slick, polished by the wind and rain.

The creature's blood trail led north, into the heart of the lava. If the creature was as smart about picking a campsite as he was about finding that ledge, this was going to be harder than Nakai had first imagined.

Nakai moved at as quick a pace as he could manage, alternately checking ahead and watching the green spots on the ground. Twice, when the creature changed direction, Nakai had to backtrack and pick up the trail. And twice he had to work his way carefully around a deep ravine the creature had obviously just bounded over. The thing could jump, that much was for certain.

And kill. Killing was its most formidable skill.

Nakai reached the ridge of one small domelike

hill and stopped scanning ahead. Suddenly he heard a faint crackling, then without warning the rock under his feet gave way with a crack louder than a gunshot.

Where he had been standing on solid rock a moment before, he was now falling.

Time slowed as the rocks around his feet shattered and he dropped.

It took an instant even to realize what had happened. It had not been something he had expected. Then it took him another instant to react.

In those two moments he was chest-high in what had been solid rock. And he was dropping fast.

Instinctively, he reached out and caught the edge of the hole with both hands as he dropped past, spacing his hands as far apart as he could. The sharp rock cut into his palms and his weight swung under the ledge, banging his knees hard on rock, sending pain streaking through his body.

His first instinct was to let go, but he didn't.

The edge held and he swung in the air and blackness of the hole, his feet touching nothing.

The strain on his arms was immense. His fingers really didn't have purchase. He had to climb up, and he had to do so carefully.

Working slowly, as if crawling out of a hole in the ice, he inched his way back up and over the edge, testing every inch before putting any weight on it.

Slowly, not even daring to breathe, he pulled himself up, moving on his stomach away from the hole, finally rolling away far enough to sit.

"Shit!" he said, taking deep shuddering breaths. "Dumb, dumb, dumb."

He had forgotten that a lot of these domelike hills were nothing more than just giant air bubbles caught in the lava. He'd been warned about lava tubes his whole life. Once he'd read that some of the tops of these hills were lava rock no more than an inch thick. Obviously he'd found one of those.

He pulled a flashlight from his pocket, lay back down on his stomach, and eased his head back over the hole, keeping his body flat and spread out so the weight wouldn't all be in one spot. The light hit jagged rocks at least sixty feet down. If he hadn't caught himself and the ledge hadn't held, he'd be dead right now, his body a broken mass of bones and flesh. And no one would ever have found him.

He eased back on his stomach a good ten feet. He had to treat this whole area as if it were thin ice. And so he had to distribute his weight, at least until he knew he was on firm ground.

Finally, he let himself stand and move down the hill. His hands were shaking more than they had in the fight with the creature. Dying in battle was one thing. Dying because he was stupid was another matter altogether.

He checked the scrapes on his legs where they had hit the wall. Luckily, nothing was broken. Next he inspected his rifle to make sure it hadn't been damaged. It also was fine.

"Lucky," he said. "Damn lucky."

He cradled his rifle, then took one last deep breath. "Let's be a little more careful now, Corporal."

His voice was whisked away by the early-morning wind into the brightening, bloodred sunrise.

25

My twin brother, Nayenez-gani, has become the hunter. He has accepted his Navajo blood. Now I must stand ready, even though I only watch from the world of my ancestors. My time of helping my brother is near. I am the brother who distracts Adikgashii so that my twin brother can kill the evil. I do not know how I will do such a task, but Grandfather has told me to believe in the strength of the story. He says that will be enough to bring me the answer I seek.

Nakai picked up the creature's blood trail on the other side of the thin dome of lava. The creature's bleeding was slowing, now down to just a drop of green fluid every few steps. The creature might have some sort of ability to heal itself, or at least stop blood loss.

For twenty minutes Nakai kept going as the sun broke over the horizon, sending clear warnings of the warmth to come. The black lava rock would act like an oven top in the heat of the day. Of course, Nakai hoped to be off this rock before that happened. He had just over an hour before the colonel started his next attack. He was either going to find the creature and report back before then, or die when the air strike hit. After what happened back in the valley, Nakai had no doubt the colonel was going to level this area.

Nakai removed the rope from his pack as he scrambled up a shallow slope. He gripped the rope in two hands, testing its thickness.

It would do.

It would have to.

When he reached the top of the slope, he paused. The view ahead was like a scene out of Arthur Conan Doyle's novel *The Lost World*. Thousands of years before, the flowing lava had forked like a river. The lava had split on a ridgeline, flowing around a small valley. At the other side of the valley, the two streams of lava had rejoined.

Nakai stared into the valley. It was like looking at a dream. The area was about ten football fields across and ten long, with plants and small trees growing all through it. In the winter the valley was a swamp, or even a shallow lake, collecting all the water off the lava around it. Now, in the summer, the trees were still fairly green, with the weeds and brush a light brown. Nakai imagined that by the end of the summer the entire valley would be brown and dried out, ready to start the entire cycle over again when the winter rains and snow came.

He had been hearing the faint sounds of chirping birds as he came up the slope, and he had attributed it to all the explosions the night before. He had been afraid that the deafening noises had ruined his inner ear, and he tried to ignore that fear.

But the ringing and chirping that he heard had actually come from the valley below. The morning light had awakened the birds, just as it did in greener places. Above the foliage a half-dozen vultures floated, circling over something just inside this edge of the trees. Something down there was dead, or very near dead. Vultures didn't circle that close unless there was food.

Nakai studied the rocks in front of him. The creature's blood trail led right into that valley.

He crouched near another collapsed lava dome and stared down. The valley was a perfect place for the creature to camp. More than likely there was still some water down there, and enough shade for the creature to get out of the sun during the heat of the day. And the lava fields made a natural barrier.

"Smart," Nakai said softly to himself. He pulled out his binoculars and studied the tree line closest to him. There was nothing in sight—no creature, and no dead body. He turned slightly, and saw a trail below him that looked recently used.

He then studied the foliage farther in, trying to spot what those vultures were circling over. It took a moment before he focused on the glasses on a human head. Even from a distance, Nakai could tell it was Sheriff Bogle's. The sunglasses and hat were still firmly in place on the head, where it sat on a stump. As Nakai watched, one of the vultures landed next to the head and pecked at it, ripping a hunk of rotting flesh from the cheek.

Nakai eased the glasses to the right a little, not

really understanding what he was seeing. Finally, the picture came into focus. It was the creature, covered in its own green blood. It was lying on its back, its arms extended as if it had fallen into that position.

Two of the vultures were now on the ground near the creature, eating at other human heads scattered around the camp. The creature didn't move.

"Is it dead?" Nakai whispered to himself, continuing to study the monster. He couldn't see if it was breathing. Could they have been lucky enough to have mortally wounded the creature in the fight?

Nakai checked his watch. One hour and ten minutes left. He had time for a closer look. Although he wasn't sure how close he wanted to get. A wounded animal was a dangerous animal, and he wasn't sure he wanted to face a more dangerous version of this creature.

Still, he had an opportunity. He would hate himself if he didn't take it. He could imagine himself hurrying back to the colonel, reporting the creature's position, and then have another debacle occur like the one last night. More people would die, and it all would be on Nakai's conscience.

He wouldn't get too close. Just close enough to shoot the thing. Not even within range of the thing's arm. Barely within sight range.

After he made sure his rifle was set for full auto, he eased down the slope, walking as silently as his grandfather had taught him. Not a stone was moved by his steps, not a twig snapped.

He reached the edge of the tree line and eased into the forest, moving slowly, carefully, listening for any sign that the creature was awake or alive. Nakai was so quiet, he didn't even alert the birds. They continued singing as if nothing were wrong.

Ten steps into the trees the smell hit him. Rotted flesh, putrefied in the heat of the last few days. Rotten human flesh.

Nakai felt his gorge rise, but he swallowed hard, wishing he had something—tobacco, Vicks, anything—to block the smell. He wanted to turn back right then, but he knew he couldn't. If that monster was just asleep, he could kill it with a full burst to the head. If the monster was already dead, he would be able to take proof back to the colonel.

And if it were playing possum, well, at least he wouldn't die under friendly fire.

Above him the thin trees seemed to tower. The dirt under his boots was soft in comparison to the lava rock. The trail wound through the brush like a snake, twisting back and forth on the path of least resistance through the trees. The creature's blood dotted the trail every few steps. And puma tracks, a few days old, also marked the trail.

The farther in, the worse the smell. With just the slightest breeze, it choked Nakai, almost making him cough. If he made it out of this alive, he was going to need a dozen showers to get this smell off his skin. It was going to take a lot more than a few showers to get it out of his memory.

He pulled out his handkerchief and wrapped it over his nose and mouth. It didn't help much, but it made him feel better as he moved forward. Five more slow, careful minutes, and he was within thirty paces of the creature's camp. Through the brush he could see glimpses of the creature, still unmoving on the ground.

Then he made a mistake.

He was staring ahead, watching the clawed hand of the creature as he stepped forward. If he had been watching where he was stepping, as he should have been doing, he would have seen the thin cord.

But he didn't see it, and his foot brushed it.

There was a loud *snap* and suddenly everything around him seemed to be moving at once. Without time for the slightest thought, he dove to the left, rolling toward the base of a tree.

He almost made it.

The spiked branch that had been held tight by the trip cord ripped into his shoulder, spinning him around and down. The pain was incredible, as if a thousand needles were being shoved into his arm and neck at the same time.

But he kept moving, rolling, until he came up sitting, back against a trunk. He still had his rifle in his left hand, but his right arm and shoulder were going to be useless to him for some time to come. A dozen thorns had torn into the shoulder, ripping muscle and tendons alike.

A low growling filled the trees. It was an unearthly sound, like nothing he had ever heard before.

Through the pain, Nakai knew he was going to die.

The creature hadn't been dead, but only resting. And now, very shortly, it would have another head for its camp. And Nakai's body would be nothing more than food for the vultures.

26

The battle has begun: the two sides are joined in combat. I can see two futures. My brother defeats the monster or my brother does not. If my brother is killed, blood will flow in the desert for years to come, for evil will walk free on the Earth.

Private Tilden rode in the open door of the helicopter back over the ground he had covered on foot twice the night before. The roar of the chopper's motor and blades made talking with the others on board impossible. The chopper was packed with troops. The base's response to the colonel was immediate. What Tilden hadn't planned on was his impromptu discussion with the brass in Washington. It seemed that a satellite had been in position the night before to pick up part of the battle. Washington had seen the destruction of the gunship before the satellite moved out of range. After the destruction of the base, the loss of the gunship was a bad sign. If this little party didn't destroy the creature, then Washington would take over the fight.

The entire U.S. military would face this thing.

Tilden hoped it wouldn't be necessary. He glanced out at the other transport choppers that were flying in formation with the one he was in. There were more troops on the transport choppers than he wanted to think about, followed by four gunships and two tanks.

This much firepower had to count for something. That creature wasn't immortal; just damned lucky and even smarter than Nakai had given it credit for being. Although Tilden had heard Nakai's warning the night before. Nakai had seen the creature survive terrific odds—hell, Tilden had seen it survive terrific odds. He knew there was a distinct possibility that today's battle would not be a rout.

He knew there was a good chance he could die today.

He hoped it wouldn't come to that.

It had been just under two hours since he left the colonel and Corporal Nakai in that valley. Now, ahead, he could see the lava field looming, a vast expanse of black stretching off into the distance. Early-morning sunlight fell across the blackness, illuminating it. The day's heat hadn't started yet but it wasn't far off, hiding just behind the remains of the night's chill like a lion ready to pounce.

The chopper turned and came in along the edge of the lava. The wind from the blades kicked up dust and dirt as the chopper neared the ground. It had landed at the edge of the battle site.

Smoke still drifted from the remains of the first

gunship. Both humvees were nothing but blackened hunks of metal.

The colonel and six others were standing in the center of the valley, facing the landing helicopters. Sentries were posted around the area. Bodies were still scattered through the brush and on the rocks. Clearly taking care of the dead was going to require some time. And it needed to be done before the day got too hot.

The chopper bumped to a landing and the sound of the engine reduced as the pilot cut the motor. Tilden dropped to the ground and, shielding his eyes from the flying dust, crouched and ran toward the colonel. A few feet away, he stopped and saluted.

The colonel returned his salute, then stepped forward and patted him on the shoulder. "Good job, Private. Were there any problems?"

"No, sir," Tilden said.

"Good." The colonel nodded. "Good."

Tilden could tell the colonel wasn't his normal self. His eyes were sunken and his voice hollow, not full of the drive and power of just yesterday. But after the colonel had lost so many men, Tilden could understand. He was still feeling shock at what had happened, but he'd had the fast hike across the desert to get his thoughts together.

Tilden glanced around for Corporal Nakai. He was nowhere to be seen.

From the other side of the chopper Major Sowel walked up to the colonel and saluted. "The first wave of reinforcements have reported for duty, sir."

The colonel returned his salute. "How long will it take the tanks to get here?"

"Another half hour," Sowel said. "Two are be-

ing airlifted in from Arizona. And we have four gunships coming in within ten minutes."

"Excellent," the colonel said. He turned away
from the major and looked at the shallow valley.
"Did you bring the body bags?"

"Yes, sir, and a team to take care of it," Sowel
said softly, clearly staring in disbelief at the scene.
Human bodies and limbs were everywhere. Not
more than twenty paces from where they were talking, a man's leg hung on a bush. The leg looked so
normal, with the boot still in place, that Tilden could
almost imagine the leg's owner sprawled on the
other side of that bush, as if he had taken a spill.

That was, he could believe that little image until
he looked at the top of the thigh, and saw the gristle,
bone, and sinews poking out of the green army fatigues.

"All right," the colonel said, his shoulders squar-
ing, his back straightening. He took a deep breath.
"Then let's take care of our dead first. We'll put the
entire unit on it until the rest of the reinforcements
arrive. Then we'll go kill the creature that did this to
us."

"Yes, sir," Sowel said. He saluted, then turned
and headed back to the chopper and the men who
were gathering there. The task of rounding up these
bodies was not going to be a pleasant one.

"Begging the colonel's pardon, sir," Tilden said,
snapping to attention.

"Yes, son."

"Where's Corporal Nakai, sir?" Tilden asked. "I
don't see him."

"He's tracking the creature," the colonel said.
"He's due back shortly."

"In the lava field?" Tilden asked.

"Yes, Private," the colonel said. "He seems to know what he's doing. And we needed the information."

Tilden nodded. "Sir, permission to follow Corporal Nakai to offer assistance."

The colonel had started to turn away, but at Tilden's request, he turned back and faced the private. For a moment he stared at him. Then he asked, "Which tribe are you from, son?"

"Zuni, sir," Tilden said.

The colonel nodded. "And Nakai is Navajo. Correct?"

"That's what he told me, sir," Tilden said.

"And you both know this desert?"

"I don't know this area, sir," Tilden said. "But I grew up in the high desert. I can take care of myself just fine."

"And you don't think Nakai can, is that it?"

"No, sir, I didn't say that," Tilden said. "I believe he can. But against that creature, any man can use help. And in that kind of lava field, it's easy for a man to twist an ankle, or break a leg. Two would have a better chance of getting back than one."

The colonel nodded. "All right, Private. Nakai said he'd track the creature's blood trail. He's been gone for over an hour now. I told him to report back within two. You follow that trail for a half hour, and if you haven't found him yet, get back here. Understand?"

"Yes, sir," Tilden said.

"Good," the colonel said. "See that you follow that order. I'm going to need you when we go in there after the creature."

"I understand, sir," Tilden said.

Two minutes later he was on the ledge where the creature had been last night. A minute after that he was following the green trail of blood over the lava field, hoping that just up ahead he would see Corporal Nakai returning. The last thing Tilden wanted to do was run into that creature, alone.

27

A true hero faces death many times, in many ways. My brother now faces it. Our grandfather says that a true measure of a soul is how it faces the moment of transition from one plane of existence to another. Many welcome the death, many cling to life with every breath. A true hero will not fear the death, and will not fight to prolong life. A true hero is focused on the task at hand, not on the results of success or failure.

"Stupid, stupid, stupid," Nakai said, scrambling to get his back against the tree behind him and his feet braced.

Blood from his ripped-up right shoulder flowed freely down his arm, dripping off his fingers. With his left hand, he yanked up his rifle, bracing it against his hip, pointing it in the direction of the creature's camp. The smell of rotting human flesh surrounded him, covering him in a sickening blanket. His shoulder throbbed in pain.

"Stupid. Stupid. Stupid."

The trees in front of Nakai moved as the creature hurried forward. When Nakai had set off the trap, the creature had roared out of its sleep, scattering the vultures. Now the creature was crashing through the brush, heading right at him. Unless Nakai cut this thing in two, he was going to die very quickly, and in a very ugly fashion.

As the creature appeared from behind a large brush, not more than twenty steps away, Nakai fired, doing his best to keep the gun level with just his left hand.

But his best wasn't good enough.

The long burst of fire missed wide, cutting down the brush five feet to the right of the creature. It roared, and raised its arms toward him as it continued to come forward. It didn't have its helmet on, and its antlike mandibles were moving, as if it anticipated a meal.

Gritting his teeth, Nakai swept the rifle toward the creature, still firing, ripping into the trees beyond like an invisible chain saw. The pain from the gun pounding against his bones sent stars through his vision, but he kept his finger on the trigger and the gun spraying bullets at the creature.

He missed.

Every shot missed.

The creature leaped up and Nakai's shots went right through the area where it had been a moment before. The creature grabbed with its taloned hands a tree limb ten feet off the ground, and swung onto it as if it were a child playing hide-and-seek.

Nakai swept the gun upward, doing his best to aim it with his left hand only, and fired again.

The creature leaped to the side—Nakai had expected it to leap closer, but it didn't—and he cut the limb it had been on into splinters.

Nakai followed with more shots, ripping up the brush, knocking down limbs of trees, covering the smell of rotting human flesh with the smell of gunpowder, filling the area around himself with a choking blue haze.

Then the gun clicked. Empty.

He had dreaded this moment. One-handed, this would not be easy.

He swung the gun down as he ejected the clip, then he braced it so that he could shove another clip in place. He brought the gun back up to his shoulder as quickly as he could. He was slow by his normal, two-handed standards, but fairly quick for one hand. The entire action took only a few seconds.

But a few seconds had been too long.

He lost sight of the creature.

He scanned the area. There was no sign of it. No green blood, no trail. Nothing.

The silence of the forest and the smell of rot dropped back in over Nakai, covering him in a layer of almost pure panic.

"Shit!" he said loud enough for the word to echo. He had to stay calm, think this through. There was no chance the creature was gone, that much was for sure. But for the moment it wasn't coming directly at him like a charging bull. Nakai knew that wouldn't last long if he stayed here.

Keeping the gun trained forward, he quickly pushed himself to his feet, using the rough bark of the tree to steady himself. Pain shot through his injured shoulder, radiating like a hot dagger through his chest and stomach. He clamped his teeth together and used the pain to force himself into motion.

He might have a chance if he got out of here. If nothing else, he could fire toward the sky to show the colonel where the creature was. The gunfire would be hard to hear from down here, but not from the lava flow.

And the colonel had to be looking for a sign.

Any sign.

Nakai turned away from the creature's camp and, staying low, headed back the way he had come. He moved faster than he thought he could. He had to get out of these trees. At least on the lava flow, he could face the creature in the open. In this brush, it could come up behind him and he wouldn't even know it.

Or come down on top of him.

A drop of green blood hit him squarely in the face an instant before the world exploded around him.

From above the rifle was yanked out of Nakai's hand, the strap broken like it was nothing more than a piece of cooked pasta.

The pain from his shoulder coursed though his entire body as Nakai tumbled and then managed to come up in a staggering run. Behind him the creature took the rifle and smashed it against a tree limb like a child angry at a broken toy. Then with a mighty leap, the creature sprang through the tops of the thin trees, landing on a large branch in a tree five paces in front of Nakai.

But the tree was old, and the huge limb rotten from too many hot summer days and swamplike winters. The creature hit it squarely with both feet, and the limb snapped with a riflelike report that echoed over the forest.

The creature was caught by surprise, its feet flying into the air as it dropped toward the trail.

Nakai didn't even slow down.

The creature landed on its back with a smacking sound and the air rushed from its chest as green blood sprayed in all directions.

Nakai wasn't about to stop to see if it was alive. At the moment he didn't figure a fall like that could kill a creature that thirty men with rifles couldn't hurt.

Nakai vaulted past the creature at the moment it hit the ground, running at his full speed toward the lava flow ahead, every step jarring pain through his shoulder.

Behind him, the creature pushed itself to its feet, a thick wheezing coming from its mouth.

Nakai glanced over his shoulder. The creature had turned around and was limping back toward its camp, letting Nakai go.

Alive!

Nakai couldn't believe his luck, but he didn't slow until he was back near the top of the nearest caved-in lava dome. Then he stopped and turned around to stare back into the trees below. He could clearly see the creature moving around its camp. Then, after a moment, it lay down next to the head of Sheriff Bogle, as if it were simply taking a nap.

"Well, I'll be goddamned," Nakai said, finally

taking a deep breath, then wincing at the pain. "The creature hurt itself with the fall."

He stood there for a moment, doing his best to catch his breath, thinking about how lucky he was. He didn't have the gun; he couldn't warn the colonel in the way he had planned, but he had escaped with his life. That counted for something.

Then, slowly, Nakai turned around and stared down into the volcanic hole behind him. And that quickly, he had a plan.

A stupid plan, he knew. He should just head back to the colonel and report the creature's position. But the creature must be prepared for that. It had to know that the army wouldn't give up so easily. It had known too many other things.

Maybe the monster's defeat wasn't going to be in a hail of bullets. Maybe the fall from the tree had been a sign. If a fall from a tree could hurt it that much, what would a sixty-foot drop onto lava rocks do for it?

The problem was how to get the creature out of his camp and into one of these holes. And that was where Nakai came in. He quickly checked his watch. The colonel would be sending in tanks and more gunships in less than an hour.

There was time.

28

Grandfather has told me my time is coming. I must watch closely, then do what I can to help my twin in his battle to slay the monster. Yet I am only a spirit, unable to touch anything on the earthly plane of existence. What can I possibly do to help my brother? Grandfather has told me I will know. He is a powerful medicine man. I must believe him.

The morning was starting to turn hot over the lava beds. Nakai finished forming his shirt into a bandage and sling for his useless right arm. Once he got the arm braced, the pain subsided to a point where he could live with it for the moment. His biggest fear was that he would hit the arm and pass out. Even willpower couldn't prevent that.

With luck, he'd have to live with the pain for the rest of the day. Without some luck, he'd be alive only another twenty minutes or so anyway.

Once he finished with the sling, he stood and checked what supplies he had left. He had a knife, binoculars, and his army-issue pistol, still in its holster on his hip. He'd lost the extra ammunition on the belt with the rifle, but there were at least seven shots left in the clip of the pistol. He also had his survival supplies, which included the most important element for his plan: matches.

Using the binoculars, he checked on the creature. The thing was still flat on its back in the forest. A dozen vultures worked on the human flesh that surrounded the monster, eating and fighting over the bits, all without seeming to wake it.

"That fall must have really hurt, huh, big fella?" Nakai said.

He put the glasses away, then went quickly to work, scavenging brush and a few sticks from the edge of the trees. He took the brush back up the hill, placing it carefully around and over the opening in the lava dome. It took him three trips down the side of the hill and back before he finally had the hole covered in such a way that it looked like a natural brush growth in the lava. He had fashioned the oldest trap in the world: a pit.

Now he had the oldest problem in the world: how to get his game to fall into his pit.

With another quick check to make sure the creature was still where he wanted it to be, Nakai walked quickly toward the right, around the forested valley. He stayed up near the dome crests so he could keep an eye on the monster as much as possible.

About a hundred paces from his trap, he dropped down to the edge of the forest, ripped a piece of cloth off his pants leg. Nakai wrapped the cloth tightly around a thick branch. He lit a match with his thumb and forefinger, then touched the flame to the edge of the fabric. He let the cloth burn for a moment before sticking it into some thick brush.

The day was already hot, and the summer had been even hotter. The brush was dry and instantly caught, almost roaring up too fast in his face.

Sweat was pouring off his body. That last was too close for comfort. He had to be extremely careful.

Now he was on a timeline, and he felt the pressure of each second. He jogged to the edge of the lava field, lighting every pile of brush he came to. It took him less than ten minutes to completely circle the valley, lighting the edges as he went, leaving only the area below his trap open and fire-free.

Then, tossing his torch into the trees, he moved back to a position right below his pit and waited.

The creature was still asleep in its camp and the vultures were still fighting over the human heads. One of them had pecked off Sheriff Bogle's sunglasses, leaving one eye socket empty, a black hole big enough to hold a golf ball.

Around the valley, the fires were raging, crackling, sending smoke and flames shooting into the air. Even if his plan didn't succeed, and the creature escaped, Nakai had managed to let the colonel know what area it had been in.

The plan worked in two ways. That was the beauty of it.

Nakai looked at the flames. They couldn't burn across the lava rock. They needed fuel. And the only place they would find fuel was in the valley. The fires had to go inward, toward the monster and its camp of rotting death.

"Better wake up there, big fella," Nakai said, staring at the creature through the binoculars. "You're going to get a hotfoot real quick if you don't."

With a squawk, the vultures flew off. They circled a few times, angry that they had lost their feast, and then the smoke drove them away.

The colonel had to be seeing this.

The fire was racing toward the creature, crackling and roaring. Heat rose and engulfed Nakai. He wiped sweat off his face. The air wavered around him as little heat pockets formed.

"Come on," Nakai whispered. "No one can sleep through this."

But it would have been wonderful if the monster could. Nakai would have burned it to death.

Of course, the instant Nakai had that thought, things changed. Finally the noise of the fire caused the creature to stir. It sat up and looked around as if it were stunned. Then it went up a tree quickly, then with a quick glance around, quickly figured out what had happened. Nakai kept an eye on it through the binoculars.

"I bet you're not a happy camper," he said.

In the tree the creature turned and looked directly at him, fixing him with those disturbing eyes.

Nakai could feel the chill of evil run through his entire body, making him shiver despite the heat of the day and the roaring fires below. He took a deep breath and then did the only thing he could think to do.

He waved.

"I'm up here, you ugly mother. Better come and get me before you become a fried piece of shit."

Through the binoculars, Nakai could see the creature square up its shoulders so that it was facing directly at him.

"Shit!" Nakai said, jumping to the right behind a large outcropping of lava rock, jarring his shoulder as he went.

The blue flame exploded where he'd been standing, sending rock into the air like a black rain.

"Pissed off, huh?" Nakai said through gritted teeth. "Good. So am I."

Carefully, he glanced over the rock. The creature was out of the tree and out of sight in the smoke and flames that now filled the small valley.

Nakai scrambled for his next position. Keeping the pit between himself and the valley, he stood up on a rock and looked down at the edge of the forest, ready to leap to a safe place at an instant's warning.

"Come on, you fat, ugly lizard," Nakai said, staring into the smoke and flames. "Show yourself."

His command was instantly answered as the creature vaulted out of the trees and started up the face of the lava, directly at Nakai.

"Now we're talking," Nakai said.

He stood his ground for a moment to make sure the creature saw him clearly, then before it could get off a shot of blue death, he dropped out of sight behind some rocks.

The creature came up the hill just as Nakai had figured it would, leaping the last twenty feet to the top.

The creature landed exactly where Nakai had

hoped, smack in the middle of the branches Nakai had fixed over the hole in the lava-dome roof.

With a huge crack, the monster disappeared out of sight, the look of surprise on its ugly face worth every ache and pain Nakai had at that moment.

"That'll teach you to look before you leap," he said, laughing to himself.

With his pistol in his left hand, Nakai moved slowly toward the edge of the pit. Not a sound came from the hole. Only the crackling fire filled the air.

Moving carefully, he inched toward the hole until he was just about to look down, hoping to see the crumpled body of the creature on the rocks below.

Instead, it came up out of the hole with a low growl, pulling itself over the edge directly in front of Nakai. Before he could move, it grabbed his leg, spilling him over backward onto the hard rock.

The creature climbed the rest of the way out of the hole and now stood above him.

Nakai could only stare into the face of death. The stench of rotting flesh covered him as the monster leaned forward, drooling. In all his life, Nakai had never been so scared.

And so ready to die.

29

My brother is about to join me in this plane. We have failed to kill the monster. I can think of no way to step into the real world and distract the evil from killing my twin. Our grandfather stands beside me, smiling. I do not understand his pleasure.

Private Tilden could see the fire ahead, the smoke filling the sky with a single black cloud. From where he stood, it looked as if the lava fields themselves were on fire, yet he knew that wasn't possible. There were some small valleys filled with brush and trees in these types of lava beds. More than likely one of those valleys had caught fire. How, Tilden had no idea, but he would wager his next month's pay it had to do with the creature.

For over thirty minutes he had been following the creature's green blood trail, never once seeing Corporal Nakai's boot print. He had also spent a short time making sure the corporal wasn't at the bottom of a caved-in lava dome. The trail had gone right over the hole, and the scattered rock looked fresh. Either the creature or Corporal Nakai had caused the cave-in, that was for sure. But neither of them was at the bottom.

Tilden stopped and studied the plumes of smoke ahead. The sun was up enough to make the black lava more like the inside of a frying pan. He could feel the heat coming up through his boots with each step he took. There was no way he, Corporal Nakai, or any other soldier could be out on this black rock during the intense heat of the afternoon. Tilden just hoped the colonel understood that fact in the coming attack.

From what Tilden could tell, the fires weren't very far away. If he could jog, he might be there within a few minutes. But jogging over this terrain was impossible. Instead he just strode out, taking long paces, forcing himself to breathe deeply, picking his footfalls, making no sound.

He was worried about Nakai. Tilden should have seen him on the way back long before this. There wasn't much time before the colonel started the next attack.

Nakai was a survivor. If he could get back, he would have.

Tilden was afraid Nakai was dead.

The fire, though, the fire gave him hope. Even if the creature had started the fire, it wouldn't have done so on purpose. It would have done so in response to something.

Something Nakai had done.

The fires were a signal of the monster's location.

And maybe, just maybe, of Nakai's location. Nakai was probably dead, but he might have been injured. He had shown an uncanny ability to survive anything that creature had thrown at him.

Tilden had to see. He had to make sure Nakai wasn't on the lava rock, crawling toward help.

Six minutes later he cleared the top of a small ridge and could see for a few miles ahead. The smoke rose upward, obscuring much of the area.

But he could see two distant figures on a dome just this side of the fire. One stood on top while the other came quickly up the side of the rock.

Too quickly.

The one climbing had to be the creature. That meant that the figure on top, more than likely, was Corporal Nakai.

Tilden stopped and pulled out his binoculars, focusing down on the two figures on the dome. As he did, the one climbing took a huge bound and then disappeared as it landed at the top of the dome.

Instantly, Tilden knew what Nakai had done. He had lured the creature into a pit, sending him to his death at the bottom of a lava dome. Nakai had somehow made the monster angry, then used himself as bait in one of the oldest hunting tricks in the book.

"Brilliant," Tilden said, laughing. "Just totally and completely brilliant!"

As he watched through the binoculars, Nakai stepped toward the pit's edge, slowly, pistol in hand. His rifle was nowhere to be seen, and even from a distance, it was clear that he was badly injured. His shirt was missing and his right arm was in a blood-stained sling. This evidently wasn't the first battle he and the creature had fought this morning.

Nakai took another step to look over the edge of the pit.

"Careful there," Tilden said to him, even though the corporal couldn't hear him from such a distance. "Don't go falling in with it."

As he finished speaking, the creature came up suddenly, like a fish taking a fly fisherman's lure out of the water. The thing must have caught the edge of the pit and pulled itself out.

Tilden didn't want to think that it was capable of jumping from the bottom of one of those pits.

The creature grabbed Nakai's ankle, sending him tumbling over backward. Then it finished climbing out of the lava dome hole.

"Shit!" Tilden screamed, yanking his rifle off his shoulder and dropping into a firing position on the ground. He was far, far too distant for any real hope at a good shot, but maybe he could distract the creature enough to force him to leave Nakai. Maybe he might even get lucky and score a hit.

But by the time he had gotten his rifle into position on a rock for the impossible long shot, he was too late.

He was too late by seconds, only seconds. But in a life-and-death battle, seconds were all that mattered.

30

It is my job as his hero twin to distract the monster long enough for Nayenezgani to fulfill the teachings of our ancestors. He has fought the battle of a warrior, yet I am only a spirit, dead at birth to the real world. Grandfather says we are linked forever. Always twins. He says that through my brother and his things, I will find a way to distract the monster. But there is nothing of my brother's close enough to make a difference except his broken weapon and his ammunition belt.

I stare at them for a moment. The ammunition belt hangs off a tree limb. The broken gun is wedged between the branches.

I stare, and then I understand.

A fresh wind breathes life into the fire, and the flames reach up toward the ammunition belt like a grasping hand.

. . . .

Corporal Enoch Nakai, lying on his back on the hard lava rock, stared up into the creature's eyes as time moved in slow motion.

The evil in those eyes was greater than he had ever imagined. The eyes narrowed. They were bright, and in their darkness, he could see his own reflection.

Tiny, small, insignificant.

The monster stared at him, and Nakai stared back. He didn't blink.

He knew he was going to die.

He knew his head was going to end up in the creature's next camp.

A trophy. He would be nothing more than a trophy.

The pistol in his left had was going to end this quickly. Nakai knew that the instant he went to raise the gun, he would lose his head. But at least he would die trying, right to the end. Grandfather would be proud.

The creature stepped slightly closer. The smell of rotted human flesh was overwhelming. The monster's armor was covered with green blood. Its breath wheezed in its throat.

The creature was hurt, too. Nakai could only hope that it was dying.

It bent over him.

With a snap, sharp blades extended from armor on the back of the alien's wrists.

Time slowed even more.

As Nakai watched, the creature started to raise its hand to strike.

Suddenly time moved at its normal pace. Gunshots filled the air, bullets ricocheting off lava rock.

Arm poised in the air, the creature looked around at the fire and the valley.

Was the colonel coming? Could Nakai really be saved by the cavalry at the last moment? He doubted his luck would last that long. Then he realized in the same instant what was happening. The fire had gotten to his ammunition belt in the valley. The heat had set off the powder in the shells.

His assailant was turned slightly, so Nakai brought up the pistol, taking dead aim at the face of evil.

Then without a fraction of a moment's hesitation, he pulled the trigger.

The gun kicked slightly in his left hand, but the first two shots found their mark squarely in the soft area just above the creature's eyes.

Nakai kept firing, pounding bullet after bullet into that ugly face.

One shot entered the mouth as the monster opened his jaws to scream.

Another shot blew out its right eye, sending green blood spraying everywhere.

The creature staggered back a step, then stood there, staring with one-eyed disbelief at Nakai.

Nakai sat up and, with careful aim, put the last two shots from his pistol directly into the monster's forehead.

The creature took another step away, and then like a giant tree, swayed for a moment before falling over backward. The body rolled over once on the rock before coming to rest on its back, its remaining eye staring at the smoke-filled sky.

Nakai stood. His legs were shaky. He stared at the creature for a moment, then at the pistol in his left hand. Then, just for good measure, he aimed the empty gun at the corpse and started pulling the trigger, letting the clicking sounds fill the air along with the crackling sounds of the fire below.

Click.

Click.

Click.

Click.

He just kept pulling the trigger, not believing the monster was really dead.

A minute later Tilden gently took the empty gun from his hand and led him to a boulder.

"I think you got him, Corporal," Tilden said quietly.

Nakai looked up into Tilden's face. It was as if the private was a hundred miles away, talking to him through a long tunnel. He didn't even know where the man came from, only that he was glad that he had come.

"Are you sure?" Nakai asked. "Are you dead sure?"

Tilden stared. And then, after a moment, he said, "You truly are *Nayenezgani.*"

At that moment, Nakai finally realized what he had done. And what he had become.

He was a hunter.

He was the monster slayer.

The past had become the present. He now understood his heritage.

He was Navajo.

And he had not become *Nayenezgani* alone.

He looked upward at the clear sky. "Thank you, Grandfather," he said.

31

My brother did not thank me. That is as it should be. He does not know of me. He will learn years from now, when he joins us.

He thanked our grandfather, who helped him more than I ever could.

Grandfather said it is time for us to move on. My brother will join us when his time comes. Then I can greet him and tell him of my pride for him. Grandfather said he will know of my pride on that day, but I will still tell him.

The colonel studied the two tanks and the four gunships that were staged just below last night's battle site. It had taken longer than he had hoped to get everything ready. The heat of the day was building, and there was no way he could send men out on that black rock. But the tanks could handle it just fine and the gunships could fly cover. They could still go, and were just about ready.

The colonel glanced up again at the ridge where Corporal Nakai and Private Tilden had disappeared. He had hoped that by now, one of them would have returned. He had given Tilden a strict order and had expected it to be obeyed. But it was now almost two hours since the private had left. Either he had disobeyed orders or something had gone terribly wrong.

Considering the number of body bags that had been airlifted out of here over the last two hours, the colonel wouldn't bet against something bad happening to those two soldiers.

The colonel took one more look at the ridgeline. Smoke rose against the pale blue sky. That smoke had to be a sign, a signal from Nakai or Tilden. The creature had to be in that spot.

If his assumption turned out to be right, and his troop managed to kill the creature, then the colonel would put in for medals for both Tilden and Nakai.

The major finished talking to one of the pilots, then turned to the colonel. "We're all ready to go, sir. Just give the word."

The colonel glanced one more time at the ridgeline, then was about to give the order when two men appeared rose against the lava rock, framed against the sun. Even from a distance, the colonel could tell it was Private Tilden helping an injured Corporal Nakai.

"Someone help them down from there," he ordered, pointing up at the ridge. Four men jumped to scramble up the side of the lava rock.

Within a few short minutes Corporal Nakai stood in front of the colonel and saluted awkwardly with his left hand. He had a bloodstained sling on his right arm and looked totally beat-up, with scratches over his neck and shoulder. Both men were covered with soot, and they smelled of smoke.

Tilden snapped off a salute correctly and smiled.

"We were about to move out," the colonel said. "I expected you back earlier."

"Yes, sir," Tilden said.

"I want a full report," the colonel said.

"Yes, sir," Nakai said wearily.

"*Now.*"

Tilden's smile widened. He glanced at Nakai. Nakai nodded.

"We found the creature's camp, sir," Nakai said. "In a valley about five miles from here."

"Great," the colonel said. "Can you give us the exact coordinates, Corporal?"

"It had a lot of human heads there," Nakai said, ignoring the colonel's question and looking disgusted. "So I burned it out."

"You what?" The colonel almost shouted. "I ordered you to not engage the creature."

"I know, sir," Nakai said. For the first time since he arrived, he smiled. "But to be honest with you, sir, it pissed me off."

"And you know how Corporal Nakai is when he gets mad, sir," Tilden said, smiling also.

The colonel gave Tilden his coldest look, but it didn't seem to faze the private. Something clearly was going on here that they weren't saying and they had better damn get to it quick.

The colonel glanced at his troops. They had gathered around the two men and were staring at them as if they had never seen anything like them before.

"So what happened next?" the colonel asked, keeping his voice even and low.

"Do you want the short version or the long version, sir?" Nakai asked.

"I want any damn version," the colonel answered. "Just get to the point."

"It fell into a pit, but climbed out," Nakai said.

"Scared hell out of me," Tilden said.

"You," Nakai said, laughing. "You were a half mile away. It was right on top of me."

"Gentlemen," the colonel snapped. "Finish this report."

"Yes, sir," Nakai said, swaying slightly, but still smiling. "Sorry, sir."

"You know how the creature likes to take heads as trophies, sir," Tilden said.

"Well," Nakai said. "We brought you something for your mantel."

With that, he reached into a pack he'd had tucked under his arm and pulled out the creature's head, holding it up for everyone to see.

"Told you that you didn't want to get Corporal Nakai pissed off," Tilden said, laughing.

Holding the head up with his left hand, Corporal Nakai was trying not to laugh along with Tilden, but without much success.

The colonel stared at the creature's head for what seemed like a long, long time. Then he did the only thing he could do.

He said, "Well done, men."

And then he too started laughing as the weight of the world lifted from his shoulders.

ABOUT THE AUTHOR

SANDY SCHOFIELD is the pen name for husband-and-wife writing team Dean Wesley Smith and Kristine Kathryn Rusch. They chose the pseudonym when they realized that their six names would not fit on a book cover.

Under the Schofield name, they have written several short stories, a *Star Trek: Deep Space Nine* novel, a *Quantum Leap* novel, and an *Aliens* novel, titled *Rogue*. They also collaborated on a publishing company, Pulphouse Publishing, Inc. That joint venture has brought them one World Fantasy award, several other award nominations, and a house full of books (including several copies of *The Best of Pulphouse* from St. Martin's Press). Kristine stopped editing for Pulphouse and for six years edited *The Magazine of Fantasy and Science Fiction*. Her work there won her science fiction's prestigious Hugo award for Best Professional Editor. Dean edited most Pulphouse projects. His editing skills have placed *Pulphouse: A Fiction Magazine* on the Hugo ballot four times. He now edits *Star Trek: Strange New Worlds,* an anthology for new writers.

Individually, Dean and Kristine have published shelvesful of short stories and novels. Dean's novel *Laying the Music to Rest* was a finalist for the Bram Stoker Award for Best Horror Novel (the only science-fiction novel to achieve that distinction). He has also sold over one hundred short stories. His current novels are *Men in Black: The Green Saliva Blues* (Bantam Books) and *The Abductors* (Tor Books), written with *Star Trek* actor Jonathan Frakes.

Kristine has sold hundreds of short stories as well as thirty novels. Her most recent novels are *Hitler's Angel* (St. Martin's Press) and *The Fey: Victory* (Bantam Books). She is writing new fantasy novels for Bantam, set in the world of the Fey, called *The Black Throne Series*.

Dean and Kristine spend their days writing and editing in their home in Oregon. They live in a house overlooking the ocean with a deaf cat, one rather dim-witted cat who acts like a dog, and four other cats who pretend to be normal (and usually fail).

The adventures continue in

ALIENS™ *vs.* PREDATOR™

One is a race of ruthless and intractable killers, owing their superiority to pure genetics. The other uses the trappings of high technology to render themselves the perfect warriors. Now, the classic conflict of heredity vs. environment, nature vs. nurture, is played out in a larger—and bloodier—arena: the universe.

ALIENS VS. PREDATOR: PREY	___56555-9
by Steve Perry and Stephani Perry	$4.99/$6.50 in Canada
ALIENS VS. PREDATOR: HUNTER'S PLANET	___56556-7
by David Bischoff	$4.99/$6.50 in Canada

And don't forget

PREDATOR™

The ultimate hunters have landed. Drawn by heat and the thrill of the chase, these alien warriors have one goal in mind: to locate the ultimate prey.

PREDATOR: CONCRETE JUNGLE	___56557-5
by Nathan Archer	$4.99/$6.50 in Canada
PREDATOR: BIG GAME	___57733-6
by Sandy Schofield	$4.99/$6.99 in Canada

- -

Buy all the *Aliens vs. Predator* novels on sale now wherever
Bantam Spectra Books are sold, or use this page for ordering.

Please send me the books I have checked above. I am enclosing $____ (add $2.50 to cover postage and handling). Send check or money order, no cash or C.O.D.'s, please.

Name _____

Address _____

City/State/Zip _____

Send order to: Bantam Books, Dept. SF 9, 2451 S. Wolf Rd., Des Plaines, IL 60018
Allow four to six weeks for delivery.

Prices and availability subject to change without notice.   SF 9 1/98

Aliens™ © 1986, 1997 Twentieth Century Fox Film Corporation.

Predator™ © 1987, 1997 Twentieth Century Fox Film Corporation. All rights reserved.

™ indicates a trademark of the Twentieth Century Fox Film Corporation.

They are the pinnacle of evolution, the universe's perfect killers...

ALIENS ™
